Slaughter Gang 2

Willie Slaughter

**Lock Down Publications and Ca$h
Presents**
Slaughter Gang 2
A Novel by *Willie Slaughter*

Willie Slaughter

Lock Down Publications
P.O. Box 870494
Mesquite, Tx 75187

Visit our website @
www.lockdownpublications.com

Lock Down Publications
Like our page on Facebook: Lock Down Publications @
www.facebook.com/lockdownpublications.ldp
Cover design and layout by: **Dynasty Cover Me**
Book interior design by: **Shawn Walker**
Edited by: **Jill Alicea**

Stay Connected with Us!

Text **LOCKDOWN** to 22828 to stay up-to-date with new releases, sneak peaks, contests and more…
Or **CLICK HERE** to sign up.
Thank you.

Like our page on Facebook:

Lock Down Publications: Facebook

Join Lock Down Publications/The New Era Reading Group

Visit our website @ www.lockdownpublications.com

Follow us on Instagram:

Lock Down Publications: Instagram

Email Us: We want to hear from you!

Submission Guideline.

Submit the first three chapters of your completed manuscript to ldpsubmissions@gmail.com, subject line: Your book's title. The manuscript must be in a .doc file and sent as an attachment. Document should be in Times New Roman, double spaced and in size 12 font. Also, provide your synopsis and full contact information. If sending multiple submissions, they must each be in a separate email.

Have a story but no way to send it electronically? You can still submit to LDP/Ca$h Presents. Send in the first three chapters, written or typed, of your completed manuscript to:

LDP: Submissions Dept
Po Box 870494
Mesquite, Tx 75187

DO NOT send original manuscript. Must be a duplicate.

Provide your synopsis and a cover letter containing your full contact information.

Thanks for considering LDP and Ca$h Presents.

Dedication

This book is dedicated to my brother, Derrick Slaughter. Rest in peace, my brother.

You'll forever live through me and the memories I'll always cherish. Slaughter Boy for life. And to my loving wife, Machumu Harris Slaughter. Thank you, luv, for holding me down and sharing your wisdom. I'm loving, cherishing, and loyal to you for life.

Willie Slaughter

Prologue

The head of the table hung up his phone. He rose to his feet and raised his champagne glass.

"Business, as usual, is taken care of, Lil Will. It's your show now, so let's hear what you have in store for this business. But, before you start, allow me to introduce myself. My name is Demetri, and this is my brother Thaddeus."

Lil Will walked around the table. "We all feel the news of Mr. Demetri stepping down today is shocking, but business must go on. Right? With that being said, everything will remain the same for now. I'll be checking in on you all to see what's going on periodically. Does anyone have a problem with that?"

No one said anything.

"Good," Lil Will said. "We all have family and friends waiting for us back home. I suggest we continue to provide for them by keeping business as business. Until our next meeting, stay safe and sound."

As they left, John and Charles walked out together. During the transition, they had taken notice of each other's concerns about it.

"What do you think, John?" asked Charles.

"Look, this kid sounds good," John replied hesitantly.

"Yeah, I know. But we been by Demetri's side for over thirty years, and he turned everything over to this guy. We don't know shit about him," John said warily.

"True," agreed Charles.

"He might take the price up on us. Then what?" John asked.

Charles paused in mid-stride. "Damn. I haven't thought about that, John. Let's just go. I can't think right now."

John nodded. "Well, we better start thinking. Shit could get real ugly, and I'm not trying to be on the bottom."

"I take it you have a plan?" asked Charles.

John looked at Charles, considering the options. "I'll call you with the details."

They jumped in their rides and left.

Lil Will and Mark were the only ones left inside of the estate with Demetri, his twin brother, and the staff. Demetri's brother had wandered off upstairs, leaving them downstairs in the meeting room.

"Mark, we got to get on the move. Phone calls need to be made to ensure every drop has been made," Lil Will said anxiously.

Mark nodded. "Let's do it."

As they were about to leave, Demetri stopped them.

"Lil Will and Mark, listen to me very carefully. Power will blind you if you let it, so keep business as business. Make good choices, because the people that you just met are important people you're going to need. It's a den of vipers. Believe me, son."

"Got you. I'll be calling upon you for wisdom from time to time," Lil Will said.

Demetri smiled at Lil Will. "Great idea. It's not like you know the people you've just met. Some of them you're definitely going to have to keep a close eye on, or things will go sour in a heartbeat."

As Lil Will and Mark headed out, Thaddeus returned from upstairs.

"Thaddeus, what do you think?" asked Demetri, thinking about the pros and cons of him leaving the business.

Thaddeus looked out the window at Lil Will and Mark as they hurried across the front lawn to the helicopter. "He's got his father's blood."

Chapter One

Dink was being Dink. He was checking the trap, making sure everybody had his paper right. Just so happened when he pushed up on Johnny Boy, shit was sour. Dink didn't think twice about hitting Johnny Boy with a left hook to the jaw.

Johnny Boy stumbled backwards while holding his jaw. "Okay, man."

"Fuck that! Where my paper, nigga?" demanded Dink as he cocked back his fist again.

Johnny Boy jumped and held his hands out in front of his face. "Dink, I'm short, bruh."

Dink frowned. "You short? Nigga, it's been three months, and you short!"

"Come on, Dink. I have a family," Johnny Boy pleaded.

Dink turned to his hitters, laughing. "You hear this nigga? I got a family too! Fuck this! Detonate this nigga!"

His hitters did as they were told.

"Fuck wrong with these niggas thinking they can take from me?" Dink said to himself while watching one of his hitters put two slugs in Johnny Boy's head before walking out the door.

As he was getting in his car, Dink's phone rang. He looked at the caller ID before answering. It was his brother, Lil Will.

"Yeah. What it do, bro?" Dink said, answering the call.

"Money," was Lil Will's response.

"True," Dink said.

Lil Will thought long and hard about what he was about to say before saying it. "Peep game. I need you to handle Southwest Georgia to Florida. Everything comes through you. Can you handle it?"

Dink sat up straight in the driver's seat, surprised to hear that his brother was giving him control. "It's about time."

Lil Will sighed, hoping he hadn't made a mistake. "I know, big bruh."

"Say no more, but check the business," Dink said. "It's getting dry here."

"I'll make something happen in a week. 300 of them will come your way. Give Teddy and Bee 100 apiece," Lil Will replied.

"Got you," stated Dink.

"It's going to be a minute before I can fly back down. I got a lot going on," Lil Will said, sounding exhausted.

"Take yo' time, bruh. I got this," Dink said with confidence.

"A'ight," responded Lil Will.

Dink, feeling entitled to know a little more than he was being told, decided to ask his brother the million dollar question. "When do I get to meet the connect? You know. Just in case some shit go sour, and one of us has to step in."

Lil Will chuckled on the other end of the line. "Stop the bullshit."

Dink's facial expression turned sour. "What the fuck you mean?"

"Just what I said," replied Lil Will. "Listen, my nigga, y'all just play your part." He hung up the phone.

Dink threw his phone on the passenger seat. "This nigga thinks he's God. Okay, I got something for his ass. I'm that nigga, fo' real," he thought out loud. He called Bee.

"What's good?" Bee said, answering the phone.

"Call everybody and tell 'em to meet up at the spot on Corn Street," Dink said with authority.

"Bet," said Bee. "Is everything good?"

Dink grinned as he swerved through traffic. "Yeah. Couldn't be better at the moment. Tell 'em to be there in thirty."

"A'ight. Love, fam," replied Bee and then he hung up.

Mike sat across from Bee, twisting a blunt of kush. After he finished, he fired it up, took three puffs, and passed it to him.

"Bee, I hear what you saying 'bout this shit with me and that nigga is bad for business, but shots been fired, my nigga," he said.

Bee hit the blunt and passed it back to Mike.

"I understand what you saying, fam. The question y'all two niggas gotta answer fo' yourselves is who you expect to front you not knowing if shit gonna be straight?"

Mike choked on the kush smoke. "Can't argue with ya, fam. Set up a truce meeting. I'll show."

"Appreciate ya understanding, my nigga," Bee said as he grabbed the blunt. "Matter of fact, we got a meeting on Corn Street in about twenty."

Mike nodded. "I'm with it, my nigga. Let's just hope Henry sees shit the way I'm seeing it. Money over ego trip."

"All fucking day," Bee agreed. "Let me make these calls."

Bee didn't bother trying to call everyone. He sent out the text to every listed contact, who hit back immediately letting him know they would be there. He called Teddy, who answered on the third ring.

"Talk to me, bro. I got the message," Teddy said as soon as he picked up.

"Where you at right now?" asked Bee.

"Fucking with Henry. Why? What's the business?" he replied.

Bee hit the blunt and passed it back to Mike before responding to his brother on the phone. "That's the business. Him and Mike gotta get this beef shit to a minimum."

"Fo' sho', my nigga," agreed Teddy. "What's the plan?"

Bee looked at Mike. "Shit, I'm with Mike now. He's willing to set aside the bullshit fo' this money."

"Hold on, bro," Teddy said.

Teddy muted his phone before talking to Henry about the situation. Henry agreed to talk to Mike, so he handed him his phone.

"Bee, what up, fam? Put Mike on the line," said Henry.

As Mike was passing him the blunt, Bee passed him his phone. "Yo. Who this?" Mike asked, putting the phone to his ear.

"It's Henry, my nigga?" Henry replied.

"What's up my nigga? My condolences to yo family," Mike said sincerely.

"Appreciate ya," said Henry.

Mike sighed. "Look, bruh. We can't survive hustling backwards, my nigga. This beef shit is outdated and over some petty-ass shit anyway. We both shot shots, niggas lost money and lives. Call that shit even."

Henry looked at Teddy, who could tell he was weighing his options. He sighed. "A'ight, homie. You right. It's dead. Let's get this money."

"Fo' sho', fam. I'll see ya at the meeting," Mike said with relief.

"A'ight. One," replied Henry before hanging up the phone.

Mike hung up and passed Bee back his iPhone. They sat in silence while they finish smoking the two blunts. Afterwards, they dipped out, heading for the meeting on Corn Street.

***

Sabrina and Sopia had met up with Kerria for a ladies' day out. Kerria had talked them into spending a day in Atlanta with her. They were in Lennox Mall, balling out at her expense.

"So, what do you think about leaving Albany, and coming to live up here, Sabrina?" asked Kerria.

Sabrina laughed comically. "I'm Good Life bound, Kerria. The money too good, and my nigga's dick is that great. Besides, Henry ain't trying to hear shit about a bitch catching grip on him. You should be asking Sopia, with her lonely ass, that."

Kerria shook her head. "I did."

Sopia stood with her hands on her hips, staring at Kerria and Sabrina. "Y'all bitches don't spare a bitch's feelings. I'm standing right here, so I can hear y'all."

Neither responded to her. They headed to the checkout counter. On their way, Sopia saw a couple of guys looking their way. Smiling, she waved at them, and they waved back.

"Damn, that nigga fine as hell!" exclaimed Sopia.

Sabrina looked around curiously. "Who? Never mind."

The guy walked over and introduced himself to Sopia. "What's up, shawty? My name is Vince."

Hearing his lingo, she found herself feeling a little girlish. "I'm Sopia. These are my home girls, Kerria and Sabrina."

Vince smiled. "That's what's up, shawty. You single?"

"Yes, she is," Sabrina answered for her.

"Damn, Sabrina," Sopia said defensively, "I can talk for myself." She looked at him and smiled. "Yes, I'm single."

He laughed. "Where ya from, shawty?"

"Albany, that Good Life," Sopia answered.

Vince nodded. "Okay, shawty. The other A."

"Yep," she said with pride.

Vince looked her up and down from head to toe. He was really liking what he saw. "Shit, shawty, what ya doing fo' the rest of the day? Maybe we can get up and do whatever's clever."

Sabrina shoved Sopia towards him. "You can take her ass on with you now. Don't worry, girl, we got ya bags. Go have a good time. Tell us how that dick is when you get back."

Sopia felt embarrassed. "Brina!"

Sabrina looked at her sideways. "Bitch, we hood. No time to act all high and mighty. Go get some you time. You'll thank us for it later. Fuck her good, Vince."

Sopia grabbed him by the arm and hurried off. The cashier tried to keep from laughing, but couldn't. Sabrina grinned at her.

"Yeah, bitches down south got flava too."

Kerria paid for their merchandise and they left. On their way out to the car, she saw Vince and Sopia pull off in a bowling ball blue donk sitting on twenty-sixes. Sabrina peeped it too.

"Maybe this little Atlanta trip was what she needed," Sabrina said to Kerria. "Because if I had to hear one more sad-ass story about that nigga Lil Will, I was gonna give her ass the silent treatment for a month. A bitch ain't got time to play a counselor without hope for her patient."

Kerria burst out laughing. "Sabrina, yo' ass silly as shit."

***

FBI Agents Wright and Dunlap were back at the office. News had hit of Agent Scott's death. With him gone, Agent Dunlap was the new commanding agent. He'd called a meeting to address the seriousness of the investigation.

After giving everyone their new assignments, he and Wright excused themselves while they discussed strategies.

They stepped outside and sat in Agent Wright's Dodge Charger.

"William, I don't think it was a good idea," Agent Wright said nervously.

"What part, Christine?" asked Agent Dunlap.

She sighed. "I think he should've allowed Scott to take him down. His crew is full of hotheads. The shit they be doing is too much to be cleaning up behind."

Agent Dunlap nodded in agreement. "I agree, and so do others who were there. Just hold on, partner. We're working on it."

***

Lil Will and Mark's flight touched down in Boston. Thankfully, they had the good sense to discard their firearms back in Texas, because the security at the airport had been tripled. One of the baggage boys walked up to Mark, insisting that he let him handle their luggage.

"Alright, youngster. Follow us," Mark said as he and Lil Will let the baggage boy take their luggage.

They made their way over to a storage, where Mark's Eddie Bower was parked. He gave the young man a hundred dollar bill.

"Thanks, man," the boy said happily.

Mark shook his head. "No, that's not for you carrying the bags. I need to know why the security is so beefed up. Do you know?"

The young man looked around, paranoid. "Man, shit been crazy 'round here. They found a federal agent dead, face first in his own piss."

He was about to hand him another hundred, but snatched it back. "What was the agent's name?"

The youngster looked at the hundred dollar bill. "Brandon Scott."

"Thank you, youngster. You can be on your way," Mark said before handing him the bill.

Without responding, the baggage boy walked off with a little pep in his step. Lil Will had to chuckle.

"Checkmate, my guy. Let's get to this money."

They jumped in the ride.

"Where to?" Mark asked Lil Will.

Lil Will looked at the time on his Rolex. It was 12:45 p.m. "Fam, let's just chill at the club, get the necessary people on line, make sure business is business, and fuck something."

"I couldn't agree more," Mark replied, putting the car in gear and pulling off from the airport.

***

The Slaughter Boyz crew had met up on Corn Street. Every brother had their personal gunman. Mike and Henry had pounded each other up and embraced, which made everyone else feel a lot more comfortable. Nobody wanted to be a victim of a stray bullet meant for either one of them.

Dink took the floor with a sense of pride. He had come to his own conclusion about his undercover takeover, but today wouldn't be the day to tell it. Instead, he smiled and did exactly what his brother had told him to do. He played his part.

"What's good, family?" Dink said, smiling from ear to ear. "If you wondering why I called this meeting, just know ain't shit gone wrong. Lil Will just gave me the keys to the city. He asked me to oversee the business from Georgia to Florida, so from here on out, y'all niggas will be checking in with me. Is that understood?"

Nobody said anything. He took it as a sign of good faith.

"A'ight. We gonna keep this shit G. Y'all know my motto. All that extra shit, talking 'bout ya short and the rest, I ain't with it. Loyalty begets loyalty with me. Disloyalty begets death. Other than that, y'all niggas have a great day," Dink stated, not looking for a response.

As they were getting ready to leave, the sound of automatics pierced the air. Everybody dropped to the floor as the slugs shattered windows and struck the walls. Mike and Henry looked at each other and nodded. They crawled on the floor over to the side door.

Mike cracked the door open and peeped outside. In his view were two gunmen with dreadlocks.

Henry, a little anxious, said. "What's up? Who you see?"

"Gotta be them Miami niggas," Mike replied, checking his clip. "I got two of 'em in sight."

Henry cocked his twin nine millimeters. "Let's clap back, my nigga."

Mike eased the door open so both of them could have a clear line of fire. The gunmen didn't see it coming. They opened fire, filling them with hot lead. Seeing their two partners down, the others hopped back in their ride and sped off.

Teddy walked over to where Mike and Henry stood right outside of the door. "So, who are they?" Teddy asked Mike and Henry.

"Florida niggas," answered Henry. "I say we don't give 'em a chance to breathe."

Mike nodded in agreement. "I'm down with ya on that, Henry."

Teddy looked from one killer to the other. "My niggas, it's good to have y'all fools working together. As far as I'm concerned, y'all do what ya do. We'll get this shit cleaned up in no time," Teddy said, smiling.

Henry and Mike made a few calls before they jumped in Mike's ride and left. Teddy strolled back inside with a smile plastered on his face that irritated Dink.

"Bruh, what the fuck is going on? This ain't the time for the joker shit!" Dink yelled.

"Since you asked so damn rudely," Teddy said sarcastically, "it's two dead niggas out front that gotta get ghost. On top of that, they're Florida niggas."

"That ain't shit to smile about," Dink shot back.

Teddy laughed while shaking his head. "Oh hell nah! I'm smiling 'cause them niggas Henry and Mike working together. What day is it, Bee?"

Bee looked at his brother questioningly. "It's Tuesday, fam. Why?"

"Fuck that shit. I'm declaring it a national holiday," Teddy stated. "Besides, everybody needs to get the fuck out of here 'til this shit in the yard gets cleaned up."

Everybody hesitated. Teddy was getting frustrated. "Ain't nobody else busting off! Back to work!"

They walked out clutching, being on the safe side. Dink, Teddy, and Bee waited for everyone else to leave before calling a cleanup crew. They sat with two blunts in rotation until they showed.

***

Vince and Sopia were having a ball. He'd taken her on a tour of Atlanta she'd never forget. Now, they chilled at his bachelor's pad, drinking Absolut and cranberry while snacking on party mix chips.

"Shawty, you good company. A nigga can fuck with ya," Vince commented.

Sopia laughed girlishly. "You good, Vince."

"Am I?" he asked.

Vince got up, walked around the table, and stood behind her. As he grabbed the cup out of her hand and set it on the dining table, he placed kisses along the back of her neck, causing her to let out a moan mixed with a sigh.

"Yeah, you good," Sopia said while relaxing beneath his touch.

She got up out of the chair and faced him. When their eyes met, their lips weren't far behind. They kissed while he undressed her on the spot. Once she was fully naked, he stepped back and looked at her as if to take a picture, which caused her to giggle.

"What?" she said, sounding seductive.

"Shawty, I'm just admiring perfection. So much shit running through a nigga's mind, shawty, I don't know what I really want to do to ya," was his reply.

Sopia cocked her head to the side. "Nigga, make it up as you go. Just come get this pussy."

And he did. He picked her up and sat her down on top of the dining room table. She leaned back as he kissed down the center of her body while massaging her breasts. When he reached her sex and tasted the sweetness and felt the heat radiating from it, he dove nose deep inside with his tongue.

Her body trembled from the pleasure he was bringing to her. She locked her legs around his neck and rotated her hips, fucking his face to the rhythm of his tongue playing inside of her. She came again and again, each time more taxing than the one before.

Feeling his own sex throbbing in need of release, he stood up straight and pulled her to the edge of the table.

Vince licked his lips while looking at her. "Damn, shawty, you sexy."

Sopia leaned back on the kitchen table and spread her legs open. "Bring that dick here, baby. Let me have it."

He allowed her to guide him inside of her. She felt so good inside that he had to close his eyes and refocus because, if not, he would've cum right then. She started grinding, pulling him deeper inside. He grabbed her by the back of her thighs and held her legs spread eagle and started long dicking her hard and fast.

Her fuck face was so amazing to him. Watching her tits bounce and listening to her whimper and moan uncontrollably motivated him to pound harder and faster. It wasn't long before he released, filling her up inside as she released her pleasure all around him. Breathing hard, he kissed and sucked on her hard nipples until his sex went soft inside of her.

Sopia held him inside of her until she grinded out another release. "Mmm, baby," she said as she came.

They sat naked at the kitchen table, enjoying each other's company. Vince had grabbed a dub of loud and twisted up two blunts. They smoked and kicked it like partners.

***

"No, Agent Wright. You'll be flying out tonight. Your flight has already been arranged. Just show up at the airport." He hung up before she could reply.

Agent Wright nodded to her partner.

"I'm going to see Demetri. If I'm not back in two days, kill him."

The blindfolded man didn't flinch or move at the orders left concerning his life. He was still unconscious from the chloroform that was on the cloth they gagged him with.

Chapter Two

Tomorrow came, and Lil Will was anticipating the call from her. All he'd done was set up more business meetings to close deals over phone instead of having to fly back down south. His right hand man Mark had text him, informing him that all shipments was on the way to their destinations. Business was on the up.

His phone vibrated, and without looking at the caller ID, he answered. "Hello?"

"Oh, hi. Is this Mr. Willie James I'm speaking with?" the female caller said.

"Yes," he replied. "Who's calling?"

"I'm Rachel Jennings," she answered, "a realtor calling on behalf of the building you were interesting in purchasing."

She had his attention. Lil Will sat up in the seat. "Is it a go?"

"Yes sir, it's a go," Rachel replied. "I'll be needing some information from you soon, like who will be on the lease. Just simple info that can be handled over phone if you're not able to be here physically."

"Thank you. Because I'm a long way from Georgia. Just text me your questions, and I'll inbox you the info needed," said Lil Will.

"Okay. Have a great day, Mr. James," the realtor said and then hung up.

He was so excited after the phone call that he rolled a fat blunt of kush and smoked alone. After the bud had kicked in, she called.

"Hey. I just texted you the info needed to send my first class ticket to. I'll see you when I get there," said Machumu.

Without giving him time to say anything, she disconnected lines. It didn't bother him. He was happy she had decided to come. Now, he was wondering what he should do to surprise her when she got there.

***

The Good Life City had turned into a warzone. The crew Ju-Ju and Tee had to set up shop teamed up with the Florida Boys, and they were on a takeover mission. They'd hit up two C.M.E. territories and a few blocks where the Front Street Boys trapped. More blood was being spilled than money being made.

Bee was out of town with his girl and Teddy was collecting some overdue dues out of the streets. Dink, on the other hand, was all business. He pulled up at a secluded area. There was only one other car there besides his, and it belonged to the man with dreadlocks propped against the driver's door smoking a Black and Mild.

"What up, my nigga?" Dink said.

His contact maintained a nonchalant attitude. "Dawg, ain't no love between us. Let's get this shit done, so we can leave the fake kicking it to the birds."

Dink laughed. "That's why I fuck with ya, nigga. Everything everything?"

The guy popped the trunk, pulled out two duffle bags, and tossed them on the ground between them.

"It's all there. All hundred and fifty G's and five bricks uncut. Now, where's my info?"

"Sending it to ya now, my nigga," he replied, pulling out his phone.

Dink texted the information to the guy's phone, which vibrated, letting him know he had an incoming message. He opened it. After reading it, he deleted it.

"A'ight, dawg. I'll get up with ya when it's over," the contact said. The guy hopped in his Chevy Caprice and pulled off. Dink picked up the bags and tossed them in the trunk. He drove off, headed for his number one trap house. So far, his plan seemed foolproof.

***

Sabrina and Sopia were back in Albany. Sopia dropped Sabrina off at her apartment. They'd made plans to visit Kerria again in the near future. To Sabrina, it was like a breath of fresh air to see and hear her friend so ready to get somewhere.

It had been months since she'd actually stayed a full night at her apartment. Since Henry was back up to speed, she didn't see a need to be his personal maid, because that's what she was beginning to feel like after his partner T moved in. And since nobody seemed to be after them anymore, she saw no reason to be subjected to his treatment.

She was so into putting up her new gear, she didn't pay attention to the safe that was sitting in the corner next to the television. She walked right past it without giving it a glance. Straight to the shower she went. In the shower, her thoughts went to the affection she hadn't been getting.

The steaming water was working miracles on her tensed body, but did nothing for the craving between her thighs. Without hesitation, she started rubbing her clitoris softly and slowly. The feeling it brought caused her to moan. She continued to finger herself, and while doing so, she massaged her breasts and tongued her nipples until they jutted out like missiles.

As she felt herself coming closer to a release, she plunged deep inside with two fingers slow stroking. She leaned back against the shower, allowing the water to run all over her body. Propping her left leg up on the side of the tub, she went deeper inside and stroked faster. On the edge, she rubbed her clitoris softly and fast in a circular motion until release. "Mmm... So much for needing a nigga for a good nut," she said to herself.

She finish showering and decided to take a nap before having to go to work.

***

Sopia pulled up at her spot, and before she hopped out of her car, drama was staring her in the face. With the heat in the streets, hood wars had become the thing. Niggas and bitches alike were out to rep where they were from. Just so happened everyone knew she was a Slaughter Boyz groupie, and the shit seemed to have come to haunt her.

Some C.M.E. girls were standing outside of her apartment building dressed to kick ass or get their asses kicked. Either way, they were there for a fight.

One of the main chicks doing all the talking walked up on her, twisting her fingers up in her face. "C.M.E. bitch! What?"

Sopia cracked her knuckles. "Bitch, take yo' dumb ass back to C.M.E. befo' you get ya ass handed to you!"

"Bitch!" the girl yelled.

The girl swung wildly at her. Sopia ducked, while at the same time, she came up out of the heels. When she stood up and weaved, she swung, catching the girl in the face with the heels. Blood flowed immediately. The rest of the girl's home girls tried to jump her, but Sopia's home girls piped up on them.

It was over. They had come for a fight, and they'd gotten one. Badly beaten, they jumped in their Honda and tore it down.

"South Side, bitch!" Sopia screamed. "Don't bring yo' ass back! Punk bitch!"

Everybody went back to doing whatever they were doing like nothing happened. Sopia grabbed her shopping bags and went into her apartment. She set the bags on the couch, headed straight for her stash, and rolled a blunt. Her adrenaline was pumping, and she needed to relax.

After smoking half of the blunt of Red Hair Cess, she picked up her phone and texted Vince.

***

John and Charles met Agent Dunlap at the seized chop shop. It hadn't been operating for over a year, so it was the perfect place to meet in secrecy. They stepped inside of the office, smiling upon seeing the blindfolded man sitting cuffed to the chair. Charles handed the agent a briefcase.

"As promised, seventy five thousand," he said.

"Keep your money," Agent Dunlap stated.

They looked at the agent, confused as to what his angle was.

Agent Dunlap sighed. He really didn't like having to explain himself, but he realized he had to. "Me and my partner are on your side in this. A street thug has no business running this business. It's bound to get messy, and some messes can't be cleaned up so easily without showing our hand."

John nodded in agreement. "We agree with you a hundred percent. It's already messy, my friend. Contacts down south tell us there's problems there as we speak. More blood being spilled than money being made."

"So, what are you suggesting we do about it?" asked the agent.

"Nothing," interjected Charles. "Let their local authorities knock their illiterate asses off. Even if our agencies have to be called in, we send the straight arrows to handle it. Our hands are washed clean of the bullshit."

"What about Lil Will?" Dunlap asked.

Charles smiled. "His ass ain't exempt. Any flake, let 'em have him. The game isn't for spot lighters. And he's too flashy, so he'll make the right mistakes that'll have his ass up the creek without a paddle."

"And what do you expect my brother's going to do when he finds out who you are?" Thaddeus had regained consciousness and overheard everything.

The agent punched him in the jaw. "Shut the fuck up, schmuck!"

"Death isn't a mystery to me. Matter of fact, killing me might prolong your lives a little longer," Thaddeus replied arrogantly.

John knelt down next to Thaddeus. "Thaddeus, why would we do such a thing? Demetri will comply. All we want is for him to take his stamp off Lil Will. After that, you're free to go back to living the rest of your life."

***

Agent Wright entered Demetri's study and stood until she was asked to be seated. She sat down with the most concerned expression splayed on her face. "What can I do for you, Mr. Demetri?"

Demetri sighed. "My brother has seemed to have come into a bit of misfortune. It seems he's been kidnapped."

Agent Wright sat straight up in the chair, looking surprised. "What? Are you sure?!"

Demetri beckoned with his hands. "Calm down, Agent. Hotheads don't come to a real solution to a problem. Yes, I'm very sure. The kidnappers called me from his personal line."

"Well, what is it they want? Ransom money? Drugs?" she asked, sounding concerned.

Demetri scratched his head. "That's the puzzling part. No, I don't think they want either. I don't think they'll kill my brother either, because it would be useless. They wouldn't get anything then."

Agent Wright nodded. "I see. What is it you propose we do, Mr. Demetri? You know my agency is at your disposal."

Demetri picked up his phone and hit his brother's line on speed dial. While it still rang, he put it on speakerphone and sat it on the table between them. The kidnapper answered.

"Hello," the kidnapper answered.

"Well, are you ready to tell me what it is you want in exchange for my brother?" asked Demetri.

"That nigga Lil Will," he replied. "You made him untouchable! Take your stamp off him," he demanded.

Demetri became furious. "That's what this is about?"

"Fucking right! Us street niggas got to eat," the kidnapper shot back.

Demetri frowned. "Street niggas? Hold on. There's no way a bunch of street thugs would know my brother or me, unless..."

He paused. If they were street thugs, there could only be one possible way for them to have known: Lil Will or Mark or both. The man on the other end realized the silence and played it to his benefit.

"Yeah, unless ya boy gave up some info," the male kidnapper said. "Of all people, you know how this game go! It's dog eat dog! You put a nigga on top who turned 'round and cutthroat ya. But fuck all the sentiments! What's it going to be?"

Demetri stared into Agent Wright's eyes, searching for answers. Seeing his dilemma, the agent nodded his approval.

Demetri sighed. "Okay, consider it done. Just send my brother back to me safe and sound."

The man chuckled. "Will do, my nigga. It's been a pleasure." The man hung up.

Demetri sighed.

"Agent, do you think it'll make a difference?"

Agent Wright nodded. "A big difference, Mr. Demetri. With everything Lil Will's crew got going on down south, business is about to get messy, and the agency can only clean up so much without having to have some people to hold accountable."

"Understood," Demetri said. "Be at the airport to see to my brother's arrival," he demanded.

"Anything else, sir? What do you suggest the agency do about Lil Will and his crew?" asked Agent Wright.

Demetri shrugged his shoulders. "Do your job. Have a great day, Agent Wright."

After the agent left, Demetri called his head of security in.

"Mr. Cobb, send out a text to all my contacts saying the halo's off Lil Will. No explanation to be given."

Mr. Cobb nodded. "As you wish, sir."

Mr. Cobb didn't leave the study. He sent the text right then and there, which was replied to immediately with the thumbs up emoji.

"It's done, sir," said the head of security.

"Thank you, Mr. Cobb," Demetri replied.

Mr. Cobb left the study. Demetri relaxed in his high back leather chair. His thoughts centered around the fact that it wasn't possible for some regular street thugs to have gotten to

Thaddeus. "It was an inside job," he said to himself. And he was bound and determined to find out.

***

Agent Wright checked the time. She was at the airport waiting on the package to arrive. All of a sudden her phone vibrated. It was a text giving her directions to where the package was located.

She walked over to the minivan parked on the side of a storage container. True to their word, Thaddeus was inside, hogtied on the floor in the back. She jumped in the driver's seat and drove back to the estate, where she hand delivered him over to his brother.

***

Lil Will and Mark were at the airport waiting on Machumu to get off the plane. Finally, she stepped into sight, and they walked over to greet and help with her luggage. Lil Will hugged and kissed her on the cheek.

"Glad to see ya make it," Lil Will said before introducing her and Mark. "Machumu, this is my fam, Mark. Mark, Machumu."

They shook hands and spoke.

"Alright, y'all, let's go. Ain't no fun hanging out at the airport," said Lil Will.

They left the airport and took her by Lil Will's place to get settled in. They asked her if she wanted to go on a tour of the city, but she declined, stating she was tired and wanted to take a nap. They left her unpacking to go handle some unfinished business.

Mark chuckled. "I see you, Lil Will."

Lil Will laughed. "What's that supposed to mean, fam?"

"Bruh, what you think I mean?" responded Mark. "What you got planned for her?"

Lil Will sighed. "I don't know yet. What do you think a nigga should do?"

"She's a cook, right?" Mark asked.

"Yeah. And?" Lil Will said.

"Shit. Give her keys to her own restaurant. Didn't you just close the deal on that spot down in Albany?" Mark said.

Lil Will nodded. "Yep."

"Let her run it. It ain't like yo' ass going back south anytime soon," Mark replied.

"For sho'," Lil Will said, taking out his phone.

He searched through his contacts until he found the realtor's number. He didn't call, but texted her the information needed to close the deal on out. She texted back to confirm the information, and he sent his electronic signature.

"Say, Mark, swing by the spot on 18th Street. Nigga gotta get his mind right befo' dropping this info on ole girl," Lil Will said.

Mark laughed and switched lanes. "Understood, my nigga."

When they made it to 18th Street, they realized something was wrong. Federal and tax agents and inspectors were all over the property. Mark hopped out and grabbed the attention of the first person who looked important enough to answer his questions. "Man, what the fuck is going on?"

"Sorry, sir," the tax agent said, "but this building didn't pass inspection and is overdue on tax payments. It's being seized until further notice. If you would like to file a complaint, I'll be glad to offer my assistance with filing the paperwork."

Mark jumped back in the car. Lil Will could tell he was mad about whatever information he'd just received.

"What's up?" he asked Mark.

"They just seized the club. Fuck," Mark said, banging his fist against the dashboard. "How the hell they do that?"

"We good on taxes and inspection?" asked Lil Will.

Mark shook his head. "Not according to what that bitch just told me. Some heavy shit going down. Hold on."

As he drove off, Mark called to his spot over on 6th Street. He listened to the person on the line, and by his facial expression, Lil Will could tell shit was sour there as well. He hung up and slammed the phone against the dashboard until the screen cracked.

"Fuck, man! What the fuck is happening?!"

Lil Will placed call.

"Hello," the man answered.

"This is Lil Will. What's going on? The feds are seizing all our properties," Lil Will said.

"I'm not entertaining this little war you all are caught up in, Lil Will. You're on your own. My advice? Tread lightly and keep your business straight," the man replied.

He hung up, leaving Lil Will in a world of thought. Mark looked at him questioningly.

"Fam, I got good news and bad news," said Lil Will.

"The bad news is obvious. What's the good news," asked Mark.

"The ball is still in our court, but it's anything goes. We ain't got no support from any agency," Lil Will replied.

Mark looked disbelieving. "Unless we buy it. What the fuck happened?"

Lil Will shrugged. "Shit happens. It always does. We got to handle shit underground. No more on the scene. After I give ol' girl the news, we're sending her ass back packing to Albany."

Mark looked at him surprisingly. "Damn, fam, you ain't gon' tap that pretty piece of pussy before she leaves? Oh shit! Duck!"

A car had pulled up beside them with a masked gunman leaning out the back window who opened fire. They ducked as the window glass shattered inward. Mark hit reverse and didn't look up until he felt they were out of the line of fire.

Lil Will sat up, panicked. "Who the fuck was that?"

Spotting the car swerving through traffic, Mark followed. They realized whoever was driving wasn't trying to get away. Their suspicion proved right when they got outside of the city. The gunman opened the back door, crouched down, and started shooting.

"Dammit, man!"

Mark slammed on brakes, put the car in park, and started dumping back. While he was having a shootout with the masked gunman, Lil Will crept up on the opposite side and let the driver and the gunman have it. He put three slugs in both of them before walking back to the car.

"Who were them fools?" Mark asked.

Lil Will closed the car door. "Fuck if I know. Dead people don't talk. Let's hurry up and send her back to Georgia. Shit is outta hand 'round here."

They arrived at his crib moments later. Mark stayed on point at the front door while he went in to help her with her belongings.

"Damn, nigga, I just got here, and you already sending me back. What's really going on?" Machumu snapped.

"Let's just say I'm being a Good Samaritan. Besides, you have your own business to open up and run in Albany," Lil Will said.

34

Machumu's eyes widened. "What?"

"Yeah. Don't worry, it's legit. It's in your name and it's paid for. Just do you," he replied.

"And what about you…us?" Machumu asked as she finished packing.

"When shit gets on the right track, I'll come get you personally. I've paid for a room for you until morning and a cab is on the way to take you there," he promised.

They hugged and kissed. He didn't want to let go of her, but Mark had yelled, telling him the cab had arrived. He walked her out and they kissed some more after he put her bags in the trunk.

"Lil Will, you better keep your promise," she demanded.

He smiled. "I'm planning on it, baby girl."

She got in the cab. He watched in deep thought until the cab was no longer visible.

"Alright, my nigga. We got to come up with a plan," Lil Will told Mark.

***

Three days passed. Dink, Bee, Teddy, Henry, and Mike were at the warehouse. The product had come in. After the shipment was carted inside and the connect left, they called their crews to break it down.

"Any word from Lil Will?" Teddy asked Dink.

"Teddy, what did I tell y'all? Lil Will told me to handle the South. All he is concerned 'bout is the paperwork being proper," Dink said irritated.

"I ain't trippin' about what he said, nigga. I'm asking out of love, bruh. This shit ain't an ego trip fo' me. I'm in it 'cause it's family," Teddy shot back.

Nobody said anything. It was two brothers arguing, so they let them argue.

Dink nodded. "That's what's up, my nigga. Let's just - "

The sound of car tires sliding on gravel caught his attention.

"What the fuck is going on outside?" Dink said, paranoid.

Mike and Henry rushed to the window and peeped out. They saw the three SUVs parked and three man crews carrying assault rifles jumped out.

"Any of y'all niggas expecting extra company?" Mike asked.

Bee and Teddy pulled their straps. Dink pulled his and hid behind the front door.

"I guess not," Mike said, cocking the 9 mm. "Henry?"

"Let's do it," Henry replied.

They put their straps up and pulled knives out before creeping outside. Their targets, they could tell, weren't professionals, so it was easy picking for them. The first two they caught slipping and slit their throats without a sound made. They'd caught one more snooping around back looking for a back door. Mike put him in a chokehold while Henry stabbed him several times in the gut.

"Three down. Three to go," Henry counted.

"No pressure. These fools amateurs," Mike said.

With the odds in their favor, they eased back inside and left the door cracked. Seeing what they'd done confused Dink.

"What the fuck ya leave the door open fo'? A nigga ain't trying to be an easy target," Dink asked.

Bee had gotten irritated with his brother. "Dink, shut the fuck up. Let 'em do what they do."

He wanted to argue, but just as he was about to open his mouth, the other three gunmen burst through the door shooting. After emptying the clips on air, they reloaded and went for the shipment, which was a mistake because Bee and Teddy gunned them down.

"Man, this shit getting fo' real," Bee said.

Mike noticed one of them was still breathing shallowly. He propped the guy against the wall and slapped him lightly. "Hey. Stay with me for a minute."

The guy's eyes fluttered open.

"There you go. Now, who the fuck sent y'all niggas on this death mission?" Mike asked.

The man shook his head. "Dawg, I ain't never met the - "

A gunshot rang out through the building. The man had a hole dead center of his head. Mike spun around and frowned at Dink. "Nigga, what the hell is yo' problem?"

Dink put his gun up. "Just finishing the job, nigga. What the fuck you mean?"

"Dink, a nigga can't fuck with you on no business! Shit to shitty and yo' ass ain't built on principles fo' shit! Man, after today, I'm done fucking with this shit if this nigga gon' be running shit," Mike said angrily.

"Word, fam. I'm with ya," Henry said.

Nobody said anything to get Mike and Henry to change their minds.

Finally, their crews arrived, and they split the work up. Mike and Henry left right after with their product, leaving the three brothers to deal with the cleanup crew. Bee shook his head in disbelief at Dink.

"What, Bee? You backing out on me too?" Dink asked.

Bee shook his head. "Nah, nigga. We family, but ya ass better tighten up."

"Dink, that was some real fuck shit you just pulled, my nigga. I ain't Bee. I'm gon' tell yo' ass straight up. We just lost a lot of fucking clientele with those two niggas walking off. Two real fucking G's, nigga. How you gonna replace that?" Teddy said.

Dink looked dumbfounded.

Teddy smirked. "I didn't think so. Fam, y'all hurry up loading that shit up so we can go. I'm sick of being around this nigga fo' the day."

"That's what's up, Teddy. Just make sho' the paperwork stay right, my nigga," Dink said, trying to save face.

They finish loading up and left. Dink waited for the cleanup crew by himself. Part of his plan was accomplished. With Mike and Henry out of the way, everything would go smoothly the next time.

Chapter Three

Demetri and his brother sat drinking hot mint tea while watching television. They hadn't discussed the kidnapping since he'd returned and probably wouldn't have breached the subject today if Thaddeus hadn't brought it up.

"You know, Demetri, I understand why you've done everything the way you did. But the one thing you were duped on was my kidnappers. They weren't just some street thugs looking for a way to eat," said Thaddeus.

Demetri looked at his twin brother. "What do you mean?"

Thaddeus sighed, remembering the ordeal. "Brother, I was smothered with chloroform. Name me one hoodlum on the streets with access to that."

That got him to thinking. It did seem a little too professionally done to have been street guys. But what was done was done.

"I see your point. Still, what's done is done. If you're gonna run a criminal empire, you gotta count the curses as the blessings," Demetri replied.

Thaddeus nodded in agreement. "I would say more than you count the blessings."

***

Machumu stood inside of the building, directing traffic. Everything she ever wanted in life was coming true. She had her own house, her own business… all that was left on her list was children and a husband. She hoped all would come with Lil Will. With that thought, she smiled and continued having things put in place.

***

Lil Will and Mark stayed ducked off at a spot that only the two of them knew about. They didn't go out; everything they wanted came like room service. Lil Will had received a text from Bee saying they needed to talk. It wasn't until after they ate he called him.

"What's good, bruh? Talk to me," Lil Will said to Bee.

"Nigga, were you thinking straight when you gave Dink the reins?" Bee said coldly.

Lil Will sat up straight in the chair. "Why you ask that? What's up?"

"In case you didn't know, this shit is a fucking warzone. Not to mention, Henry and Mike ain't fucking with us anymore because of this nigga's dumb-ass ways."

His brother gave him the rundown on everything that was going on down south. It took everything in him to keep from blowing his cool, but he maintained through the whole ordeal.

"So, as you can see, shit been fucked up since Dink started smelling his shit again," Bee replied.

Lil Will took a deep breath and sighed. "Dammit bruh. My bad. Y'all niggas just do what you can. As long as the paperwork good, I'll be able to keep y'all straight, fam. But whatever you do, don't get caught slipping by any means."

Bee frowned. "State ain't giving us no problems."

"Take my advice, fam. Oh yeah. Look out fo' ole girl fo' me. She just opened the spot up," Lil Will said.

"So that's yo' piece? Nice, fam. I got you," Bee promised.

"Love, bruh," Lil Will said and then hung up.

He threw the phone on the sofa. Mark fired up a blunt and passed it to him. He hit it twice and tried to pass it back, but Mark refused.

"Nah, homie. That's yours. I got my own."

Mark fired up his. They smoked, drank, and called up a couple of groupies to slay. When they arrived, it was a party, nothing going on but stripping, sucking, and fucking.

***

Chill had gotten a call from Henry. He wanted to meet up at The Fox. He was on his way when a truck hit his car from the blindside. The initial hit didn't kill him, but the two slugs to the dome did.

The truck driver ran back to his truck and drove off. He drove a couple blocks over and hopped out and into the ride that waited.

"Business handled?" the driver asked.

"Yeah, that nigga's dead," he replied.

"Money in the plastic bag on the backseat. Where you want to be dropped off, my guy?" the driver asked.

He looked at the time. "Shit, might as well hit The Fox."

"A'ight," he said and then drove off.

They swerved into the right lane, heading for the club. When they got there and inside, the first person both men noticed was Henry, who was quickly joined by Mike. The two men avoided making any kind of contact with them.

While they were trying to blend in with the crowd on the dance floor, a fight broke out between hoods.

"A nigga catch hell enjoying hisself 'round this bitch! Where that nigga Chill?" Mike asked Henry checked the time. It wasn't like his cousin to be late. He hit his line. All he got was voicemail.

"Something ain't right," Henry said, concerned. "Let's peel!"

Henry and Mike left the club. On their way to the east side, they passed what seemed to have been a car accident. Henry felt a tug in his gut and slowed to a stop.

"What up, Henry?" Mike asked.

"Hold up. I'm trying to see something," Henry said.

He watched as an officer picked up a phone. As he was about to put it in an evidence bag, Henry hit a number in his contacts. Just as he thought, it was Chill.

"What the fuck?" Henry said angrily.

"What? What's up?" Mike said with panic in his voice.

"Bruh, that's Chill," Henry said.

He jumped out and ran over to the officer handling collecting evidence. "Excuse me, Officer. What happened here?"

The officer looked at Henry. "Are you a next to kin of the victim?"

Henry nodded. "Yeah. Tony Holt's my first cousin. What happened?"

The officer stopped writing on the notepad. "Well, at first we thought it was a freak accident. You know, like drunk driving. But the bullet holes in his head say different."

Henry couldn't even respond. He ran back and hopped in the car. As they drove off, he filled Mike in on the details.

"Who you thinking?" Mike asked.

"I give less than a fuck. All these niggas suspect."

"Shit, my nigga, pick the first victim, and let's fuck their world up."

Henry shot back, "I got some shit to check out real quick."

Henry went by Sabrina's apartment building. Seeing the light on, they got out and he knocked on her door. They heard footsteps hurrying towards the door.

"Who is it?" Sabrina yelled.

"It's Henry, Sabrina!" Henry yelled back.

She opened the door and stepped to the side. They walked in. Henry looked around. "You got company?"

"Nobody but Sopia. We were 'bout to hit the club," Sabrina said before speaking to Mike. "What's up, Mike? Haven't seen yo' ass in a minute."

Mike laughed. "I'm good. Where Sopia at?"

"Upstairs," Sabrina said. "Sopia!"

She came running down the stairs in a bra and panties. Instead of running back up to get dressed, when she saw Mike, she walked on down, straight up to him, and hugged him. "What's up, Mike?"

"You. You still chasing dreams?" Mike asked comically.

She giggled. "You want to find out?"

Henry walked back into the living room. He saw the interaction and decided to join the fun. "What's up, Sabrina? Why don't we give them a minute?"

"Who needs a minute? We real homegirls. If y'all fucking something, it can go down right now," Sabrina said.

Sabrina pushed Henry back on the couch next to Mike. Both women stripped down to their birthday suits. They got on their knees in front of them before massaging their dicks right up out of their pants and giving them head. They bobbed up and down, taking it deep throat.

They got up off their knees and straddled them. They moaned, screamed, and fucked them unmercifully. When it was over, they ran back upstairs, leaving Mike and Henry to do whatever they were about to do.

"You find what you needed?" Mike asked.

"And some. Let's go. That bitch knows how to drive a nigga crazy," Henry said.

***

Dink met up with his contact again.

"Dawg, that shit went straight south, my nigga. Luckily, the other shit panned out, or we wouldn't be having this meeting," his contact said angrily.

Dink looked at him sideways. "My nigga, don't blame me fo' ya mans and 'em fucking up. Anyway, that li'l bit been handled. Next shipment will be easier to drop in on."

"Well, ya cut ain't what it would've been, dawg. But it's forty percent of all we hit fo'," he said.

Dink grabbed the bags and left without exchanging any other words. At the stop sign, he texted him the info needed to do the next job.

***

Agent Dunlap was grinning from ear to ear. They'd hit Lil Will and his crew hard for business properties. The only thing they hadn't touched was the drug trade, and that's only because it would be obvious since they already knew every route.

He walked out of the building over into the overhead parking garage to his car. As he approached the black sedan, his Nightrider ringtone went off.

"Agent Dunlap speaking," he answered. "How may I help you?"

"Just shut the fuck up and get in the car. No sudden moves, or your wife and kids get it," the man's voice on the other end said harshly.

Agent Dunlap's heart dropped to his feet. He swallowed hard.

"Okay. Whoever you are, you got my attention. Please, don't hurt my family."

"Just get your scared ass in the fucking car. We'll talk about who dies and lives when you reach the destination," the caller said.

"Where?" Dunlap asked nervously.

"Old junkyard outside of town in fifteen minutes. Don't be late, or bye-bye little ones and wifey," the man said promisingly.

The line went dead. Agent Dunlap thought about calling his partner, but didn't. The voice made it clear he was being watched. He jumped in the car, and as soon as he stuck the key in the ignition, a sharp pain crept up the back of his neck and everything went black.

The figure, dressed in dark blue slacks and a matching turtleneck, hopped out and pushed his unconscious body over to the passenger side. He cuffed him to the door brace and drove off. Seven hours later, he pulled up at the security post.

"Damien," he said as he flashed his ID.

The guard looked at his ID closely. "Circle around back, sir. The place is already prepared."

He drove through the security gates and straight to the back, where a group of shotgun houses stood. Two of them had armed guards standing outside. He rolled down the driver's side window.

"Damien," he said to one of the guys.

The man pointed. "Fourth house down. Everything you need is already inside."

By the time he pulled up to the house, Dunlap woke up. He looked around panicky. "Man, who are you? Where are we? What have you done with my family?"

Damien responded by holding the agent's head still while ejecting him with the needle, which caused him to go back out.

Damien honked the horn once, and three armed guards came out and took the agent inside. After they secured his restraints on the metal bedsprings, one of them sprayed a sheen on a cloth and put it under his nose, causing him to regain consciousness.

"Listen. Whatever's going on, I'm pretty sure it's a misunderstanding that can be easily fixed. No need for getting carried away," the agent said with fear radiant within his voice.

The armed guards didn't respond. One of them sat in a chair with a gun on his lap, and the other two left and stood on post. The man who had driven him there circled back around front and hopped out. The front door opened before he got the chance to knock.

"Mr. Damien," the butler said, holding the front door open, "you're expected. Come in, sir. Follow me."

Contemporary classical music filled the hallway. The butler led him into the den, where his employers sat enjoying the music, eating fruit off a silver platter. One of them stood and shook his hand.

"Well done, Damien. Your father and I are proud of your successes," the man said proudly.

"Thank you, Uncle," Damien replied.

"No. Thank you," his uncle replied. "Sit. Have some fruit with your family."

He sat down and grabbed a handful of grapes. They made small talk about the well-being of his mother and other siblings. After an hour or so, he looked at his Rolex. "I must be going. Is there anything else?"

His uncle nodded. "Yes. Have the agent's family terminated."

He pulled out his phone and, while texting, he asked if they wanted the termination filmed, to which they answered yes.

"Okay. Consider it done. The video will be sent to your private sector. Anything else Uncle? Father?" Damien asked sincerely.

"Not at the moment, Damien," his father replied. "Go enjoy the fruits of your labor. And be sure to give your mother and everyone else our blessings."

Damien nodded. "Will do. Father. Uncle."

He left carrying two briefcases containing a million apiece - one for his team and the other for him and whoever he cared to share it with. For him, it was always family first. Although they were filthy rich from years of being heads of drug lords, his principle was that you could never have enough.

The two gentlemen had a laptop brought into the den. Both had to enter passwords in order to open the private account documents. Once opened, the live streaming of the termination appeared. It was gruesome.

The children got off easy with bullets to the back of their heads. Their mother, on the other hand, was literally dismantled. They shot her up with a full syringe of adrenaline before chopping her up limb by limb with axes. At the sight, one of the gentlemen had to close his eyelids.

"Oh my," Thaddeus said, placing his right hand over his heart. "I can't say I miss such days."

Demetri chuckled. "That's the whole point of climbing to the top. Oh well. Let's send this to the agent. Might as well let him see what his foolishness has caused him before he dies."

They shared the link.

The guard inside the room with Agent Dunlap heard the laptop beep. He downloaded the shared link.

"You have a message," he told Dunlap. He turned the screen so he could see it.

The agent's body shook violently from fear. "Oh my God! Not my wife and kids! Why? Why not just kill me?"

"Be careful what you ask for, Agent."

The screen turned black. Then two faces popped up. Seeing them, his expression was horrified.

Seeing his fear only caused them to smile.

"Did you not think your voice was unrecognizable?" Thaddeus asked the agent.

Dunlap shook his head. "You got the wrong guy!"

Demetri waved his hand before the camera. "Oh save it, Agent Dunlap. Your friends, John and Charles, are right beside you. And yes, they gave you up in exchange for the lives of their children. And, yes again, their wives got the same treatment as yours. One actually got worse."

The agent broke down in tears. One of the gentlemen frowned.

"Why does everyone play tough, but when their dirt comes back to cover them, they go all soft? Anyone you would like to give up that we don't already know about?" asked Thaddeus.

The agent didn't respond. His thoughts were elsewhere. Vengeance. He wanted to eradicate Lil Will and his whole family, and he put the plan together immediately.

"What does it matter? I'm a dead man anyway," Dunlap said in defiance.

"Maybe, maybe not. Your other accomplices are still alive because they're loyal to three things. Themselves, money, and children," Demetri replied.

"Why wasn't I given an option?" the agent asked.

"Your line of work says you know better than to get involved with certain things, Agent Dunlap," was Demetri's response.

"You're right, and I'm sorry. No harm was ever gonna be done to him. All we wanted was to remove what we considered a threat to all of us. As you know, they're running things into the ground in the south," Dunlap stated defensively.

Demetri sighed. "All y'all had to do was come to us with your concerns. Everyone would've had the chance to cast their votes, and none of this would have to happen. We're businessmen. And what's bad for business would've been taken care of in a decent manner."

"Your kingpin was planning a coupe. Everyone was about to be cut out of millions. How do I know? One of his brothers has been playing double agent, not knowing the people he's supplying with the info worked for Brandon Scott's brother Ju-Ju. So we get all the intel and product," stated Dunlap.

The gentlemen's facial expression went blank. The newfound information was interesting and valuable.

"Okay, Agent Dunlap," Thaddeus started to say. "If we decide to let you go, what is it you plan to do?"

"Kill the sons of bitches who gave me up, and bring Lil Will down before too much damage is done to this business," he answered without hesitation.

"Interesting, but not good enough. Goodbye, Agent Dunlap," said Demetri.

The armed guard took the farewell to be the signal. He stood over the agent and put two slugs in his head. One between the eyes and the other at the temple. Shortly after, gunshots could be heard coming from the other houses.

***

News reporters were everywhere on the scene. One was reporting live.

"We're live where Federal Agent Dunlap's family was found brutally murdered. His two daughters and son were shot execution style, and his wife was butchered. The troubling part of all this is that two other government officials' families were found in similar conditions."

Agent Wright took out her private phone and made a call.

"Hello, Agent Wright," the man said. "How're you doing today? And thank you for providing us with the intel."

"No problem, sir. I already have the evidence to pin this on the fall guys. Will there be anything else?" she asked.

"No. Goodbye," he said.

The line went dead. Agent Wright gave orders for her team to gather whatever evidence they could find and meet her back at the office. Once in the car, she got control of her breathing and heart rate. She swore to herself never to play with her family's lives again.

Slaughter Gang 2

Chapter Four

Lil Will and Mark stayed in tune with the news. So much crazy shit was going on around them. They didn't know whether to count the deaths as blessings or curses. Mark had left for the day, feeling the need to check in on his family. Lil Will already knew what was up on his end, but he did decide to give Machumu a call.

"Hello," she answered.

"Hey there, sexy. How's business life going?" Lil Will said.

"Great, but it would be greater if you were here," Machumu responded.

"Greatest. Because I would feel at my best being next to ya right now," he replied, feeling where she was coming from.

"Speaking of which," Machumu began. "When will you be, Mr. James?"

"Kind of hard to say with all the crazy shit happening 'round here and down there," Lil Will said.

Machumu sighed, thinking about half of the killings being reported on the news. "You ain't lying. These niggas killing each other without reason."

"So I hear. Ain't nobody pushing up on you wrong, are they?" Lil Will asked out of concern.

"No, baby. I'm good. Listen, I got more customers than workers at the moment. I gotta go. Bye," she said and then hung up.

Lil Will turned his attention back to the news just in time to see the breaking news report. He damn near jumped out of his seat when his picture flashed across the screen. He turned the volume up.

"Breaking news! We have reports from the Federal Bureau of Investigation office that says Willie James, also known

51

as Lil Will, is the leading suspect in the ring of murders! Leading investigator Agent Wright says they have concrete evidence that supports the allegations against Mr. James, and a warrant has been issued for his arrest! There's also a seventy five thousand dollar reward for anyone who could give the whereabouts of the assailant at large!"

Before Lil Will could hit him on speed dial, Mark was already calling. "Fam, you seeing this shit?" Mark asked.

"Yep. A nigga got to get the fuck on," Lil Will replied.

"Where to?" Mark wanted to know.

"A nigga always wanted to live the vamp life, so Cali, my nigga," was Lil Will's answer.

"I'm on it," said Mark.

"Appreciate ya, bruh. You know you got to run this shit while I'm hiding out. Make sho' ya run it how you see fit, fam. Choose Bee or Teddy fo' ya contact in the South. Don't send shit else through Dink," Lil Will instructed.

"I got you, bro. Let me set this shit up for you can bail before shit gets too real 'round here. I ain't trying to find out how far them bitches we been trimming 'round with loyalty goes. A hungry bitch will do the most," Mark said.

"True. A'ight, my nigga. Get back at me ASAP," Lil Will replied.

"Bet. One," responded Mark.

They hung up.

Immediately, Lil Will started packing. He knew time wasn't on his side. As he walked through the kitchen, he heard a knock at the front door.

He paused to gather his composure before creeping up and looking out the peephole. It was pizza delivery. The young lady knocked again. He slid a hundred dollar bill beneath the door.

"You can just leave it beside the door and keep the change," yelled Lil Will.

The delivery girl picked up the money. "Okay. Thank you."

He watched as she set the bags down, picked up the money, and left. Quickly, he opened the door, grabbed the food, and closed the door and locked it. It was the most paranoid he'd been in his entire life. All he could think about was not going back to prison.

"Open the door, fam. It's Mark," Mark said.

Relieved to hear Mark's voice, Lil Will opened the door.

Mark stepped in and asked, "You ready?"

"Hell yeah. Let's go. We can eat this shit while we riding," Lil Will said, anxious to leave the area.

"Fo' sho'. I got a private flight lined up fo' ya. The pilot is already fueling up, so by the time we get there, he'll be ready to take flight," Mark said.

They took every precaution on their way to the airstrip. By the time they got there, the food was gone. Before Lil Will got on the plane, they embraced.

"My brother," Lil Will said while patting Mark on the back.

"The same love's here, fam. We'll be up soon. It's a hundred thousand in the briefcase, and I'll be sending more when you need it," Mark said.

"Love, fam," Lil Will replied.

Lil Will jumped on the plane. Mark watched until they were in the air. Back in his car he called Teddy, who picked up immediately.

Teddy answered. "Man, talk to me. What the fuck is going on with bruh?"

"That's what I'm calling you 'bout. From now on, you my go-to guy. If you ain't available, then it's Bee. Dink's outta the picture," Mark said.

"The last drop is already up in smoke," Teddy informed Mark.

"That's what I need to hear, fam. And from here on out, we'll deal personally. Meet me at whatever destination I text you with the paperwork," Mark stated.

"I'm feeling ya business ethics, my nigga. Is bruh a'ight?" Teddy sounded concerned.

"Yeah, for the most part. Fam laying low like an alligator in the swamp. When it's his time to come up, he'll come up. As long as we're eating, he's eating," Mark said.

"True. That's what it do, my nigga. I gotta go collect the rest of the paperwork," Teddy said.

"Do that, and let me know when you ready to make that move," replied Mark.

"Fo' sho' fam. One," Teddy stated.

They hung up.

Mark's mind flipped to straight business mode. Nobody was after him, so he knew he had to keep it that way. All throughout the rest of the day, he made calls, establishing allies and cutting ties with others. He even called Demetri, who picked up on the second ring.

"Hello," Demetri answered.

"This is Mark," said Mark.

On the other end of the line, Demetri smiled. "Yes, I remember you, Mark. What can I do for you?"

"We need to talk," said Mark, businesslike.

"I'll have a personal helicopter pick you up in about three hours," Demetri said.

Mark looked confused. "How, when you don't know where I'm at?"

Demetri laughed a good-natured laugh. "Mark, return to the airstrip you just came from, and a chopper will bring you to me."

He hung up before Mark could respond.

Mark turned around, heading back to the airstrip. Just as Demetri had said, when he arrived, a helicopter awaited him with armed men dressed in suits. One of them shook his hand.

"Good day, sir! Let's go," the bodyguard yelled.

They boarded the helicopter and took to the air.

They arrived at the estate at first dark. Mark was shown into a study and asked to be seated. He complied and relaxed.

Shortly after, the twins walked in and sat down.

Thaddeus leaned back in the chair, looking all business. "What can we do for you, my friend?"

Mark kept his business composure. "Y'all know what's going on with the business. And I'm pretty damn sure you know about the feds being after Lil Will."

Thaddeus nodded. "Yes, but what's any of that got to do with us?"

Mark sat up straight in the chair and looked Thaddeus in the eyes. "I'm taking over for Lil Will while he's in hiding. I've already - "

"Established new contacts and changed the way business will be handled in the South," Thaddeus cut him off. "Yes, we are very aware of your smarts, Mark. You have our support, to a certain degree. We'll make sure nothing goes wrong with business, but it's up to you to keep yourself alive."

Mark nodded. "Understood."

Demetri sat up straight in his chair and stared into Mark's eyes. "Words from the wise. People don't last long in this business being a public figure. Make yourself a ghost."

"Definitely understood. I guess I'll be going. Appreciate your support," Mark replied sincerely.

"No, Mark. Thank you. And you shall remain our guest for the night. A guestroom is already prepared. Rest well, because tomorrow, it's down to serious business," said Demetri.

The butler came in and showed Mark to his room. It was laid with everything needed. A fresh set of bath cloths and towels, soap, shampoo, deodorant, and a navy blue pinstripe suit were laid out on the bed. He looked back at the butler.

"On the house, sir. Businessmen dress the part. Goodnight, sir," the butler said and then left him to shower and rest.

***

Teddy hit Bee up and they met at Machumu's new spot for breakfast. She tried to serve them on the house, but they declined, saying, "Money ain't made by being nice." It was something she understood. After their food was brought to them, they ate and chopped it up.

With the new news Teddy filled him in on, Bee felt a lot better about business.

"That's fucked up 'bout bruh, but fam just did the right thing. So, what we looking like?" Bee asked.

"Oh, we good, bro. I'll hit the connect up and let him know I'm ready to move 'round seven," Teddy replied.

Bee smiled. "That's the move."

"How do you feel 'bout fucking with Henry and Mike on this big boy business tip?" asked Teddy.

Bee nodded. "Nigga, we need solid niggas like 'em on the team."

"My thoughts too, bruh. Set up a meeting with 'em to see what's up. I'm gonna get ready to handle this paperwork," said Teddy.

"Bet. I'll call you after we've met. Knowing them, they ain't got no problems dealing strictly with me and you," Bee reminded Teddy.

They finish eating and left a major tip on the table.

Machumu smiled. She knew they were looking out for her on account of Lil Will. That made her think about him.

***

Dink was scoring big. He was capping off of his brother's business and his own. His trap had become a million dollar spot. He was waiting on his man to show up when his phone rung.

"Yo. What up?" Dink answered his phone.

"I'm pulling up now," the caller said. He hung up on the other end.

Dink posted near the trunk of the car, watching as he pulled up and got out. There was no exchange of words. They exchanged goods, and both men went their way.

That didn't bother him. He preferred it like that. It kept business as business.

***

Teddy met up with Mark in North Carolina. They ate lemon-peppered lobster and crab and drank Coronas before they found a secluded spot to conduct their business. To the public eyes, they looked like they were having a lawyer/client visit. Mark was in his suit, and Teddy was in casual slacks and a long-sleeved smoke grey silk shirt with a black and grey tie.

Teddy followed Mark to the docks. There, he grabbed the duffle bags out of the trunk and put them in the trunk of Mark's ride before jumping in on the passenger's side.

"All the paperwork straight. I got to give it to ya. I like ya movement. Our business relationship gon' be solid," commented Teddy.

"I know, homie. Just do me a favor. Don't tell anybody shit about me. Matter of fact, don't show yo' hand either. Play the game the way it's meant to be played. Change up yo' dress code, make smart legal investments, and stay off the scene. Let yo' team move for you, fam," Mark said.

Teddy nodded. "Word, bro. I got you. I'll be sho' to preach the same message to my niggas."

"Good. Your shipment coming by boat. It's going to arrive two days from now. I'll text you the info and codename you going to need to get the pick-up. 'Til then, stay safe and sound, fam," said Mark.

"Fo' sho'. Tell bruh I said what's up when you hear from him again," replied Teddy. Teddy hopped out and trotted back to his ride.

Mark waited a few minutes after he left before he pulled off and into the flow of traffic. He was already feeling his new role.

***

Henry and Mike met up with Bee at Machumu's restaurant. All of them ordered the special for the day plus extra fried potato logs. Once the waitress left, Bee was ready to conduct business.

"If you wondering why a nigga called y'all, don't stress it. This what's going down. We outing Dink's dumb ass on business. Me and Teddy gon' be handling shit from now on with the major shit. We want to know if y'all wanted to get down with the team. So, what's up?" said Bee.

The waitress came back carrying a tray with their plates on it. Mike helped her put it on the table. She thanked him and left.

"What are we looking at?" Mike asked Bee.

"Mike, it's us, fam," Bee said. "We get the work, split it up even, and the numbers we bring back to the table to go back is even. All gain is ours. What you make is what you make. Straight like that."

"Alright, my nigga," Mike said with a serious look, "we in. But, I'm telling ya now, if yo' brother gets in the mix, y'all can cancel us out. And we ain't giving up shit."

Bee held his hand out. They shook on it. "Deal, fam. Let's enjoy this meal. These bitches can cook their asses off in this spot."

They ate, and as usual, left a tip bigger than the cost of their meals altogether. Bee sent his brother Teddy the text to confirm their meeting was successful. When he received it, he smiled.

***

Sopia chilled at Sabrina's apartment. After their little fuck fest with Henry and Mike, she was loose and with whatever. They sat watching television when a special news report came up. Her jaw dropped when Lil Will's picture flashed across the screen.

"Girl, turn that shit up," she told Sabrina.

Sabrina grabbed the remote and hit the volume button. A federal agent was speaking.

"The assailant, Willie James - also known as Lil Will - is still at large. He is the alleged murderer of a judge, a district attorney, and a federal agent along with their families. We're offering a hundred thousand dollar reward for anyone who will give us his whereabouts. Just call this number on the screen. Thank you."

Sabrina looked at Sopia, whose mouth was still open.

"Bitch, snap out of it. That's a dead nigga now. I wish I knew where his ass was. Hundred thousand, and I'll leave the fucking country for good."

***

Agent Wright met with her contact in Georgia. The man with the long dreadlocks handed her a set of keys.

"It's all there. Everything except the money I get to keep."

"Forty percent, right?" she said, checking to see if he would lie.

He nodded. "Yep. I gotta say, this is the most cutthroat guy I've dealt with. He's so bent on running shit it's pathetic."

Agent Wright allowed herself to smile. "Well, let him stay pathetic. It keeps us paid and well informed."

"How much longer before the big bust? I'm ready to call it," he asked her.

She thought for a moment. "Let me check with some of our colleagues, and I'll get back to you. Until then, make your money."

The guy strolled back to his ride and left. Agent Wright tossed the keys to the van to the slender-figured light-skinned woman.

"You know what to do. I'll see you back at the office Friday."

Without responding, she trotted to the van, got in, and drove off. Agent Wright took out her phone and dialed a number. The line connected after the first ring.

"Hello, Agent. What news do you have for me today?" the male voice on the other end said as he answered.

Agent Wright looked around, making sure nobody else was in earshot. "The information Dunlap gave up checked out. The product and money are on their way to the destination."

"That's great news, Agent. Is there anything I can do for you?" the man asked.

"Well, my son's birthday is tomorrow, and I promised him we would go somewhere special for a week," she said.

"Oh, a paid vacation?" the man said with enthusiasm. "How does Italy sound? It's nice there this time of the year."

"I'm sure he would love that, sir," she replied.

"Well, Italy it is. I'll have a private plane fly you roundtrip. Be ready to go in the morning," he said.

"Thank you so much. How will I ever repay you?" Agent Wright stated happily.

"Continue being loyal, Agent. Loyalty is all I ask in exchange for anything. Goodbye," the man said before hanging up.

She drove straight home and started packing. Her husband and son asked her what was going on. Her only reply was to tell them to get some rest because tomorrow would be a busy day for them.

***

Henry was on the phone with Sabrina, trying to find out what her plans were for the day. He and Mike were en route. She had told him to come find out instead of hitting her line.

"Bye," Sabrina said comically before hanging up on him.

"Well damn," Henry exclaimed.

He hung up the phone. As they were about to get in their cars, he told Mike to follow him. They made it to Sabrina's apartment. She came to the door butt naked. "Y'all know what time it is."

They walked in and sat on the couch. Sopia came sashaying down the stairs naked. She stood next to her homegirl. "Y'all niggas want a show?"

Mike nodded with a blank expression on his face. "Do what ya do."

Sabrina started tonguing Sopia down while rubbing between her thighs. She was instantly turned on and started moaning, kissing, and rubbing on her too. Down on the floor, they grinded pussy to pussy until they both climaxed. Mike and Henry felt like they were in sex heaven.

They watched them lick and tongue each other down until they couldn't take it anymore. They grabbed them from behind and commenced to long dicking them hard and fast doggy style. It was hard to tell who moaned and screamed the loudest.

As they were about to cum, they pulled out. Sopia and Sabrina turned around and sucked them until they came, allowing their cum to run down the sides of their mouths.

Sabrina smiled. "Yeah, y'all niggas like that, don't cha? Don't go soft on a bitch yet. Y'all gotta work this pussy overtime tonight."

Henry and Mike rolled Sabrina and Sopia over on their backs and mounted them like they were mounting horses. They started out slow grinding until they felt their sexes rock up inside of them. Then they bucked on them like fucking might go out of style tomorrow, so give it all you got tonight. After round for round and pound for pound, Mike twisted up three blunts while the girls washed up.

Once they came back down, still naked, Mike fired up with Sopia laying across his lap, and Sabrina across Henry's. They were indeed living the good life.

***

Lil Will was paranoid, but still living the California vamp life. He found himself smoking so many different grades of chronic and sexing so many different mixtures of broads. The last one he hit told him she was African, Asian, and Latino mixed. He was living the dream.

He was smoking a stick of Grand Papa Purp when his phone rang. "Hello," he answered with caution.

"What's up, Mr. James?" the feminine voice said.

It was Machumu. Lil Will lightened up. "Missing you. What's up?"

"Taking care of business," she replied. "Had some free time, so I had to see if you were reachable. No need to lie because I've watched the news."

"Yeah, about that bullshit," he said coldly. "I didn't do it. Them dick-sucking feds set me up."

"You don't have to convince me," she said sincerely. "I'm on your side. Matter of fact, this call has lasted too long. You never know if they've tapped phone lines or not. Goodbye, baby." Machumu hung up.

It was clear to him she wanted a life with him just as bad as he wanted a life with her. He leaned back in the chair, enjoying his thoughts and the Purp, when a slug tore through the door. Quickly, he hit the floor and pulled his gun.

"Yeah, I believe this is the spot the bitch said he's at," a man said quietly.

"I hope so," another man replied. "A nigga needs to collect that check. They did say dead or alive, didn't they?"

His partner nodded. "Hell yeah. That's - "

Lil Will let off two shots, hitting both men with face shots. They hit the floor. Without hesitation, he packed up his gear and hit the alleyway to the other spot Mark had set up for emergency purposes like this.

***

The boat had come in, but before Teddy walked down to the docking area, a van pulled up and a woman leaned out the window calling the code name. He stopped and waited for her to catch up with him. When she did, she handed him the keys to the van.

Teddy took the keys. "What's this for?"

"Consider it a show of good faith. Besides, you need the van to load the shipment into," the woman said.

They walked together down to the waiting boat. Once the boatman saw the lady, he waved them over. The three of them carried the product from the boat and put it in the back of the van. Once that was done, she held out her hand.

"Your car keys. Trust me, with what was already in the van, you can buy another one."

Teddy gave her the keys. She waited on him to drive off and for the boatman to be on his way before she left.

Teddy drove a new route to the new location only he, Bee, Mike, and Henry knew about. Once he got there, he called them on a conference call, telling them the whale had come to shore.

Thirty minutes later, they pulled up. Inside, Teddy opened the back door of the van. "Actually, it's more here than what it's supposed to be. Even some paper. A show of good faith. We split the extra and make extra."

Nobody had a problem with it. They sat for hours breaking the work down evenly, putting it in duffle bags and into the trunks of their cars. It was midnight when they finished. Mike and Henry rode together, and Teddy rode with Bee, leaving the van with the keys in it inside the spot.

***

Dink was at The Fox, drunk as usual, sitting in VIP and spending money like crazy. He grabbed one of the dancers on the ass and squeezed it. She slapped him across the face.

"Bitch!" He backhanded her so hard she hit the floor.

Immediately, the bouncers came in and asked him to leave nicely.

Dink brushed them off. "My nigga, fuck y'all and that bitch! I ain't going any fucking where! Make me!"

One of the bouncers went to snatch him up, but when he grabbed him, Dink hit him across the head with a bottle. He fell to the floor, bleeding out. The others rushed him. They picked him up, carried him to the door, and tossed him outside. He hit the gravel face first.

Dink got up, staggering. "Y'all bitch-ass niggas done fucked up! Nigga, I'm Dink! I run this shit!"

They didn't pay him any attention. The bouncers went back inside.

Dink staggered over to his ride. When he got in and looked in the mirror, he snapped.

"Oh hell, fuck nah! These bitches gon' pay fo' this shit!" he yelled.

His face was all scratched up from the gravel. Dink grabbed his Tech nine millimeter and went back in the club. Without warning, he let loose.

"Die, motherfuckers!" he screamed as he sprayed the club up.

After emptying the clip, Dink ran out and left. Good thing was, he was drunk, so his aim was low. Several people got injured, but nobody died.

***

Mark had stayed at home most of the day, surfing the web for new business sites. He'd found a couple and sent emails to the realtors handling the properties. Lil Will had contacted him earlier, telling him what had happened. He sent him fifty thousand to a private account he could access from a phone.

He'd laid down to take a nap when the phone rang. He didn't want to answer, but he did just in case it was important. "Hello?"

"Just calling to congratulate you on your successes. Keep things exactly like they are," the caller commended Mark.

"I plan on it," Mark replied.

"I'm having a little private get together this weekend, and it would be great if you could make it. We'll give you a code name, so no one will know your position," the man said.

"Count me in then," Mark replied, accepting the invitation.

"Great," the man said enthusiastically. "Be at the airport bright and early. I prefer for you to beat the crowd here so we can chat about being successful."

"I'll be there," Mark said, sounding promising.

"Goodbye."

He hung up and Mark closed his eyes.

Morning came quicker than he would've liked it. Fresh out the shower and into a Hilfiger business suit, and he was on his way to the airport. He boarded the private flight without going through any security checks, which let him know the ball was definitely in his court.

A couple hours later, they touched down at the airstrip right down the road from the estate. Demetri himself had come to meet him with six well-trained bodyguards. They shook hands before getting in the Hummer. On the way over, they talked politics and religion, and to Mark's surprise, Demetri was an atheist.

They arrived at the estate and were escorted in by the guards. The two men joined Thaddeus at the built-in sports bar. They all sat and chatted while drinking champagne,

"As you can see, Mark," Demetri began saying, "this business isn't all that hard. All you have to do is be a ghost to the streets and a family to the public and at home. And never forget where you come from."

Mark chuckled. "That's easy not to do. I appreciate all the wisdom."

"You're welcome. But the pleasure is all ours," Demetri replied. "Nobody likes seeing something they built with sweat and blood destroyed. As it stands, you're the savior of our organization. The least we can do is provide you with the wisdom to survive in a den of serpents."

The butler came through the door and announced that the other guests had arrived.

"Okay," Demetri said. "You're no longer Mark. You're our niece's husband, Brad. Okay?"

Mark nodded. "Got it."

They walked down the hall, talking and laughing like they'd known each other for ages. When they reached the grand dining room, everyone who was seated stood. Demetri beckoned with both hands for them to sit back down.

"Everyone, I would like to introduce you to my niece's husband, Brad. He's a successful legitimate businessman back home," said Demetri.

They all spoke, and Brad nodded in response.

"Good," Demetri stated, clasping his hands together. "The gist of this meeting is to feast. So, let's eat, drink, and be merry. Business isn't up for discussion amongst us who all do our part."

Everyone ate and drank their share. Casual conversation was partaken in. Brad stayed at the right hand side of Thaddeus with Demetri to his left. He was observing the interaction, and being where he was from and the people he was used to dealing with made it easy for him to tell the phony from the real sitting around the table.

Demetri noticed his watchful eyes and smiled. He excused himself and asked Brad to join him. Out of earshot, they stopped.

"Okay, Nephew, what did you see?" asked Demetri.

Brad thought for a moment before he answered. "The balding gentleman four chairs down is just as fake as he wants to be. Him and the two ladies across from him must've come together because they're all into his act. They was hoping the get together was for business, but seeing that it isn't, they're hoping to steer the discussion somewhat that way."

Demetri nodded approvingly. "Great observation, Nephew. Anything else?"

"Yes," he replied. "One of the women is strapped."

Demetri's eyes went wide. "What? How do you know that?"

"She's uneasy. That's a sign of concealing," Brad said.

"Hmm..." Demetri said in deep thought. "Let's get back to our guests."

They walked back inside where the others were still talking boisterous.

"Ladies and gentlemen," Demetri said with a smile, "all will remain here for this night. Your sleeping quarters have been prepared, and I'm sure you'll find everything you need inside. Have a wonderful night. Brad, Thad, please join me in my study."

Everybody said their goodnights before the butler began escorting them one at a time to their quarters.

Demetri, Brad, and Thaddeus watched them from a security camera screen inside of the study.

"Now let's see how good your observation is, Brad," said Demetri.

He zoomed in on the room where the lady he'd said was armed entered. And just as he'd stated, she was strapped. They watched as she lifted her skirt and pulled the baby three-eighty out of her pussy. All Demetri could do was shake his head. "Such a pity. Go disarm her and bring her to me please."

"Yes sir," Brad said and walked out.

Demetri and Thaddeus watched as Brad casually walked down the hall and into her room. The lady smiled at him lustfully. He played along until he was in striking distance, where he caught her with a solid right to the jaw, knocking her out. He retrieved the weapon, tossed her over his shoulder, and brought her directly to the study.

"Hand delivered, Uncle," Brad said.

"Thank you. Take her out back," said Demetri.

The guard, who wasn't there before Brad left, picked her up and left the room.

"The other two will have a rude awakening," Demetri said coldly. "Tomorrow, after the others are gone, I'll show you what happens to disloyal people like them. Until then, get some rest, Nephew."

Brad found himself in the same room from the first visit. He showered and went to sleep.

The next morning, Brad was awakened by the sound of cars leaving the estate. He jumped up, got himself together, and headed out to meet Demetri and Thaddeus, who he found standing out front.

"Did I oversleep?" he asked as he walked up.

Demetri shook his head. "No, Nephew. You're right on time. Let's take a walk."

Demetri, Thaddeus, and Brad walked around back.

It was Brad's first time seeing the shotgun houses. They walked into the first one, and inside was the one guy, the balding gentleman he'd pointed out.

"Hey there, friend," Demetri said politely.

The man was clearly afraid. "What's going on? Tell these fools to release me!"

"Okay," he said and turned to the guard. "Release him," Demetri commanded.

The armed guard slit his throat from ear to ear. Seeing the job done, they walked to the next house, where both of the ladies were strapped down in chairs.

"Lily and Triece," Demetri said, sounding surprised.

Lily had already accepted her fate, but Triece, on the other hand, hadn't. "Listen! It wasn't our idea! We're sorry!"

Demetri looked on Triece with pity. "What did you expect to gain?"

"We just need more business," she pleaded. "Don't do this! Please!"

Thaddeus, not trying to hear it, nodded to the guard, who screwed the silencer on the pistol and shot them each twice in the head. Again, they walked out.

Outside, Demetri took a deep breath of the fresh morning air.

"That's how you deal with such messes," Demetri told Brad. "Never get blood on your hands unless it's absolutely necessary, which would be never as long as you remain a ghost."

Brad nodded. "Understood, Uncle."

"Great," he said in a serious tone of voice. "Now, you must be on your way. We'll be sure to keep in touch on a regular basis."

The three men shook hands. Brad hopped on the helicopter that flew him back to Boston.

Willie Slaughter

Chapter Five

Everything was going great for Teddy and his crew. In his eyes, The Slaughter Boyz were definitely back on top with the new and improved management. They were at the hospital with Bee. His girl had gone into labor, and he'd reached out to them and they'd come.

She had the baby boy and named him Y'Kee Dontavious James. Bee's mama was there to pray over him, and Bee nominated all of his partners as godfathers of his newborn. After the celebrating came to a calm, his mother pulled him out of the room and asked if he had heard from Lil Will.

"Mama, I know you've seen and read the news 'bout what's going on. He's good. We get money to him once every two weeks. Don't worry, Mama. We got him," Bee said.

"What about Dink?" she asked out of concern.

Bee sighed out of frustration. "Yeah, the streets are talking. Mama, he's too far gone. We tried to straighten him up, but he's bad for business, so we let him do him."

"That's understandable, baby. Y'all boys be careful. Mama appreciates everything y'all do. At the same time, Mama wanna see her boys safe. Ya hear?" his mother replied.

Bee nodded. "Yes ma'am."

"Good. Now, let me go back in here with my grandbaby. All y'all hoodlums can leave now," she said.

Bee laughed and hugged his mother. He pounded up Teddy, Mike, and Henry before they left.

***

Dink had laid low for a day after the shooting at The Fox. Knowing he had to do some due collecting, he hopped up and drove over to his trap. His right hand man, Trav, was sitting on the porch sipping on a forty when he got there.

"Trav, what's good, my nigga?" said Dink.

"Us. Fuck them. What's up?" Trav replied.

"Came to collect," Dink responded. "What ya got fo' me?"

Trav looked at Dink sideways. "Nigga, with all the gunplay and bullshit ya got going on, it's been hard on the yard. Shit been moving slow."

Dink shook his head, knowing he was right. "Alright, cool. Just give me what ya got."

"Hold on fo' a minute."

Trav stepped in the house. When he didn't come right back out, Dink cocked his nine millimeter and crept through the door. He watched as his partner separated money, putting some in a safe and the rest in a duffle bag. It was on his mind to bust him, but he thought better of his situation and crept back outside and sat on the porch.

He came out and dropped the bag on the porch between them.

"Eighty G's, fam. I'll have the other seven-five befo' the night over."

"A'ight, my nigga. Stay true."

He grabbed the bag and left. At the stop sign, he pulled out his phone and made a call.

"Yeah. What up, dawg?" the man answered.

"Everything everything?" asked Dink.

"Fo' sho', dawg," he replied. "Everything panned out. You know where to meet me." He hung up.

Dink made a U-turn and drove to the spot. After waiting for about twenty minutes, his connect pulled up and hopped out, smiling.

"Dawg, that last lick was on the up. Here ya go, my guy."

Dink grabbed two of the three duffle bags. They carried them to his car and put them in the trunk.

"That's four hundred fifty thousand, dawg. Plus nine bricks of that pink shit," his contact said.

"Nice doing business with ya, my nigga," said Dink. "I got some shit fo' ya to hit tonight. I'll text ya the info."

The man nodded. "A'ight dawg. We'll get up."

Dink got in his car, grinning like the fucking devil while he texted him the next lick. Once he received the okay, he drove off. In his mind, he had built it, and he would destroy it and rebuild it again. Just with a new right hand man to hold it down.

***

Night came, and Trav had called a freak over he'd served earlier. She might've been on the blow, but the bitch was still fine. She was what he called a conservative, social, functioning junkie. Job, owned her own shit and never came up short.

She'd already got him off with the head game. Instead of treating her like the freak she was, he started making love to her. He even ate the pussy and sucked the cum right up out of her when she climaxed.

She moaned and squirmed from the pleasure.

"You like that, girl?" Trav asked.

"Yeah, baby! Yeah," she moaned and screamed.

He kissed his way back up to her lips, where he tongued her down while sliding inside her. She moaned and so did he while they slow grinded together to Lorenzo's, *You Ain't Had No Loving 'Til You Had Me.*

The sight was almost ridiculous to the gunman watching from the door. Really, he didn't want to kill the woman, so he waited in the shadows inside the room until they finished. Besides, he thought, the nigga deserved to get his last nut. On top of that, the bitch was a fine redbone. No need to kill a piece of pussy he might get to test drive sooner or later.

Finally, the tempo changed. He couldn't figure out who moaned and screamed the loudest between them. He definitely made a mental note to find out who she was. Trav short-stroked her faster and faster until he came.

He rolled off top, breathing hard. She got up and got dressed while he opened the safe beside the bed. He took out some money.

"Here yo' pretty ass go," he said as he handed her the money. "Ten bands. Just don't give that pussy to anybody else."

She took the money and smiled. "Boy, this is yours. Same time tomorrow?"

He slapped her on her soft round ass. "You know it, girl."

She looked surprised. "Goodnight, Travis."

She walked right past the gunman and didn't see him. Or maybe she didn't care. Either way, it was good for him.

He watched Trav twist a blunt, fire it up, and lay back on the bed, smoking.

"Bitch-ass nigga, don't move," the man said demandingly.

Trav sat straight up, which was the wrong response. The gunman put three in his chest before walking up on him. "Damn, nigga, you don't understand English? I said don't move."

He put the fourth slug in his head. Thankfully, the safe was still open. He opened the duffle bag he carried and threw everything inside. He was about to leave when he thought about the woman, whose DNA would definitely be found on the scene.

He sighed. Checking around, he realized the stove was a gas stove. He turned every knob to the max, filling the air with the propane fumes. He grabbed a strap he saw next to the bed and put it in the microwave and set the timer on two hours. After he started the timer, he crept out through the back door and jumped in his car, tossing the duffle bag in the backseat before driving off. He pulled over and waited two blocks down to make sure everything went as planned. As soon as he looked at his watch, smoke and fire filled the air in the direction he'd just come from. Satisfied, he pulled off.

***

Teddy, Mike, Henry, Bee, and T were chilling at Henry's spot. The money had been made three times over and they were counting up the go-back paperwork. After they finished, Teddy pulled out the new briefcases and put the money in them.

"Alright, y'all. We on the up. Everything everything? Y'all good?" asked Teddy.

Everybody nodded.

"Yo, fam, I got an idea," T said in deep thought.

"What's up, T? Tell it," replied Teddy.

"We should start a record label. Slaughter Boyz Inc. Easy legitimate money," T said.

Everybody paused in deep thought.

Bee smiled at the idea. "Fucking right, my nigga. What ya say, bruh?"

Teddy nodded. "A'ight, T. Yo' ass running it. Find out the works on it."

T smiled. "Young G, I already done that. That's why I brought it up. A nigga did a stretch. Y'all don't think niggas sit in prison steady fucking up, do ya?"

They all laughed. Once they parted ways, Teddy sat in his car on the phone.

"Yo, what's good, bro?" the man asked.

"The whale went back out to sea. We caught all the fish, and now we outta bait," said Teddy.

"You know the bait store I run. It'll be open tomorrow at six," the connect replied.

"Bet," Teddy said. "I'll be there, and I'll bring you a nice plate of fried fish and grits, my nigga."

The connect laughed. "Yeah. Give ya mama my love."

"Fo' sho', bruh," said Teddy.

They hung up, and he pulled into the moving traffic.

The woman just smirked. Agent Wright whistled.

"That's some cold shit. Anyway, what we looking like?"

"Mostly uncut," he replied. "But some stepped on too. Even some high grade grass and ninety thousand. And yes, that's after my cut. The keys are in the van."

"Good. Good," Agent Wright replied.

The woman walked over to the van, jumped in, and drove off.

"Nice doing business with you, but your services are no longer required."

She pulled out the pistol with the silencer and put a bullet right between his eyes. Agent Wright walked up on his body and put two more in his chest. Before leaving the scene, she collected the casings and dragged her feet over their shoe tracks. Knowing what to do was an advantage she had.

***

Mark and Teddy sat inside a coffee shop in North Carolina, sipping coffee and talking about sports. After they finished their cups, they left.

"All there, fam. Here ya go," Teddy said.

He handed him the keys to his car, and Mark gave him his. "The whale is on its way," Mark informed him.

They went their separate ways.

***

Dink's trap was back to booming. His new right hand man had called him, letting him know he was out of work. He tried to contact his connect, but he wasn't picking up his line. And, for some reason, the shipment that was coming through Lil Will had stopped, something he chalked up to the news reports. With nowhere else to turn, he called his brother.

Bee answered. "What up, bro? Talk to me."

"Bee, I'm outta work, and my supplier ain't answering his line," Dink said.

"Nigga," Bee snapped, "you act like I'm doing any better. Ain't shit come my way since you stopped getting the drops."

Dink held the phone out from his ear frowning. "Damn. A nigga gotta go fuck with some outta town niggas to get some work."

"That's how everybody else surviving," Bee replied.

Dink sighed. "Alright, bruh. I'll get up with ya."

He hung up. Dink didn't knew his next move. He had the money, but no connection. He grabbed his gun and left.

He pulled up on the Westside. A couple of hustlers were out trapping. He jumped out and strolled up on them. One of them noticed him. "Dink, what up, my nigga?"

Dink walked up smiling. "Surviving, nigga. Lay that shit down."

He pulled out on them. They were stunned. He shot one of them in the leg. He fell, screaming in pain.

Dink held them at gunpoint. "Nigga, ain't nobody playing with y'all punk ass! Come up off it! Dope, money, and jewelry, nigga!"

They stripped themselves down, laying everything on the pavement.

"Kick bricks, nigga! Get somewhere befo' I change my mind and bust yo' dumb ass," Dink snapped.

He helped his partner up and they scrammed.

Dink picked everything up and trotted back over to his ride and peeled off. All that day, he pulled armed robbery after armed robbery. By the time he made it back to the south side, he'd hit a nice lick for seven and a half bricks, some crumbs, and sixteen thousand. He took the work straight to the trap and dropped it on his crew.

***

Bee was out with his baby mama and son. His life had taken a turn since his son was born. They sat in Machumu's restaurant, enjoying a meal and each other's company.

"Dee, close your eyes," he demanded.

Dee looked at him curiously. "What is it, Bee?"

"Just do it," Bee said.

She closed her eyes.

He took the small jewelry box out of his pocket before kneeling down in front of her. "You can open your eyes now."

She opened her eyes, and when she saw the diamond ring, she started screaming.

Bee stared into her eyes. "Will you marry me, Dee? I promise you I'm leaving this shit alone."

"Yes! Yes!" she screamed.

He put the ring on her finger and hugged and kissed her. He ordered them a red velvet cake to celebrate. After they ate all they could eat, he left a tip and they left.

On their way out, a guy bumped into him.

He mugged Bee. "Damn, my nigga. Open yo' eyes."

Bee threw up his hands. "My bad, my nigga."

The guy looked Bee up and down. "I know my, nigga."

Bee smirked. "It's all good, fam."

Bee and his family walked on out.

The guy watched as they drove off and pulled out his phone. The line connected. A man answered, saying, "Yo, what up?"

"I just bumped into that nigga's li'l brotha. His ass gon' get got," the caller said.

"Where that nigga Dink at? That's who we want. His brotha ain't did shit," he tried to explain.

The man watching Bee shook his head. "Man, fuck that. If we can't get that nigga, we get the next thang to him."

The guy on the phone said, "Nah, my nigga. Call that shit off."

"It's too late. Money in the bank. Nigga already on him," he said and then hung up.

***

Bee stopped over at his mother's house to tell her the news.

She started crying on the spot and hugged her son. "Boy, I'm so proud of you!"

He hugged her back. "Yeah, Mama, I'm 'bout to let the streets go too. It's all straight for my family."

Ruby lifted her hands high above her head. "Thank you, Jesus! Y'all hungry?"

Bee shook his head. "No ma'am. We just finished eating."
His phone rang. It was a business call.

"Excuse me. I gotta take this call," he said.

He walked out on the front porch and answered the phone.
"What's good, fam?"

"Man, ya brotha Dink came through my trap and laid some of my young niggas down," the caller answered and said.

"What?" Bee stepped off the porch and went and sat in his car.

"Yeah," the man began saying, "the nigga been pulling capers all fucking week. Watch yo'self, my nigga."

The advice was good, but too late. By the time Bee looked up, two gunmen stood in front of his car with assault rifles and emptied the clips. The voice on the other end kept saying "hello" and calling his name, but he didn't respond. He knew Bee was dead.

His mother and fiancée came running out of the house. Seeing the car windows shot out, they immediately started screaming. His mother saw her son's bloody body and fell to her knees. Dee hurried up and called Teddy and told him what happened.

Teddy wasn't trying to believe what he was hearing. "Slow down, Dee! What's going on?"

"They killed Bee! Some niggas just killed Bee!" Dee yelled at Teddy.

"Y'all go in the house! We're on the way," said Teddy before he hung up.

He called Mike and Henry. Ten minutes later, they were all sitting with his mother, Dee, and the baby, who all cried.

Teddy was heated. "Did y'all see anyone?"

"No," Dee replied. "We were inside. When his phone rang, he stepped outside."

"Mike, go get the phone before the police get here," Teddy said.

Mike went and grabbed the phone.

Teddy told his mother to wait fifteen minutes before she called the cops. They jumped in their rides and left. Back at Henry's spot, they called the last number on the caller's ID.

The man answered. "Damn Bee, why you didn't say something when I was hollering ya name through the phone? A nigga thought you was dead."

Teddy was pissed. "Fuck nigga, my brother is dead! Now who the fuck are you?"

There was silence for a second. "Aye, my nigga, I called to warn fam 'bout the shit. His blood ain't on my hands."

"Then who the fuck did it?" demanded Teddy.

He gave them the rundown on the shit Dink had been doing. "Yeah, my nigga, the shit had gone too far befo' a nigga could stop it."

Teddy rubbed his head, nervous and mad. "Fuck!"

Teddy hung up. He looked at Mike and Henry, who both had tears and murder in their eyes. They shared his pain. He called Lil Will.

"Say bro, we got a serious problem," Teddy said in a serious tone of voice.

Lil Will was concerned. "What's wrong?"

The tears were burning in Teddy's eyes. "Bruh, Dink's bitch ass just got Bee killed."

"What?" Lil Will said in disbelief.

Teddy sighed. "Yeah. My nigga had just proposed to Dee, and he was stepping away from the game. Niggas offed him right in front of Mama's house."

Lil Will was furious. "Nigga, just chill and keep taking care of business. I'm on my way."

Willie Slaughter

Chapter Six

The shipment came and so did the same woman in another van. They made the same exchange, but this time she smiled at him.

Teddy looked at her questioningly. "What?"

"You have an extra passenger," she replied.

"Who?" Teddy asked curiously.

"Me," came a man's voice.

Teddy turned around to see Lil Will. They embraced.

"Bruh, what the fuck?" Teddy said, his voice full of emotion.

"Y'all just keep handling business. I'm here to take care of the G shit," Lil Will said.

The woman did the same as last time. Once they left, she left. On her way to the helicopter, she had a call come in.

She answered the phone. "Yes sir. It'll be done by tomorrow morning. Okay, sir. You too, sir."

***

Agent Wright walked out of her office, feeling good. As she sat in her car, the passenger side door opened and the woman got in and closed the door.

"Drive, Agent," she demanded.

Agent Wright looked at her out of the corner of her eye. "Where to?"

The woman sighed, shaking her head. "Never mind." She judo chopped Agent Wright in the throat.

Gasping for air, Agent Wright leaned forward. She shot her twice right under the chin. Getting out of the car, she left a device on the passenger seat.

After she was thirty yards out, she pressed the detonator and the car exploded in flames. She made the call. "It's done," she said in a professional tone of voice.

The man smiled. "Thank you, Niece. We're expecting you at the estate soon."

"I'm on my way now, Uncle Demetri," she said. They hung up.

Demetri made another call.

The person picked up. "Hello? Special Agent Sarah speaking."

"Hello, Special Agent Sarah," Demetri said. "How're you this morning?"

"No complaints. Looking forward to my promotion soon," Sarah replied.

"You just got it," Demetri responded. "Now, make the evidence go away."

"No problem," she stated and then hung up.

***

Special Agent Sarah had received the call about an explosion that had taken place in the agency's parking port. She walked out acting as if she was surprised and concerned. The other agents were standing around looking confused. She could tell they were more scared and paranoid than confused.

"Agents, we must ask ourselves, is this a tragedy or is it karma? What you all are failing to realize is, the agents and their families who have been murdered lately were all a part of an ongoing private investigation. Yes, they were the ones being investigated for certain compromises within the agency. Now that all of them have met their demises, more than likely by the hands of those they were in cahoots with, the private investigation is over," she said, easing the tension.

One of the agents raised a hand. Sarah quickly acknowledged her. "Yes, Agent Harris?"

Agent Harris put her hand down. "What about the manhunt for Willie James? Is that a part of this special investigation?"

Sarah nodded. "You're correct, and the manhunt ends with the death of Agent Wright. To confirm your suspicion, the so-called evidence that points Willie James out to be the murder suspect is all frivolous and planted by Agents Wright and Dunlap, who are also deceased."

"So, we can get back to doing FBI work and stop chasing personal vendettas?" questioned Agent Harris.

Sarah nodded again. "Correct, Agent Harris. I'll be giving everyone's new posts and assignments tomorrow at zero eight hundred. You are all dismissed."

***

Everyone was at Bee's funeral. Teddy, Henry, and Mike sat next to his mother and Dee, who held their son on her lap. Dink sat three rows back, feeling the heated tension from others. The reverend had preached the sermon, and everyone stood and walked to the casket to pay their respects.

Dink was the last one to step up to view the body of his brother, whose death he was responsible for.

"Damn, Bee, I fucked up. I'm sorry, li'l bruh," Dink said, his voice full of emotion.

The people behind him were murmuring about something. He really didn't care that they were talking bad about him.

As Dink turned to walk off, a fist slammed hard into his jaw, knocking him off his feet. He was so dazed he couldn't see who his attacker was, but the voice wasn't mistakable.

"Nigga, you the reason li'l bruh in that casket," Lil Will stated angrily.

Lil Will started stomping him out. Teddy, Mike, and Henry grabbed him, pulling him off Dink, who struggled to recuperate from the assault.

Dink got to his feet, holding his jaw. "I'm sorry, bruh. I didn't mean fo' it to happen like this."

Teddy frowned. "What, nigga?"

Now it was Teddy's turn. He decked Dink with a left. Then it turned real bad for Dink. All four of them ended up on him like bees on honey.

Their mother Ruby stood up and yelled, "Lord Jesus! Y'all stop! Just stop it! Now!" They stopped.

Their mother walked over in between them and helped a badly bruised and bleeding Dink to his feet.

"Thank you, Mama. I'm sorry," Dink said.

As the tears flowed from her eyes, she slapped him across the face.

"Boy, sorry ain't gonna bring my son back! The only reason I stopped 'em is I don't want any of 'em going to jail for killing yo' no good ass!"

Dee put a hand on Ruby's shoulder and guided her back to her seat.

Lil Will had murder in his eyes. As he looked at his oldest brother, all he could think about was death.

"Bruh, ain't the feds after you?" Dink asked Lil Will. "You need to lay low. I'll take care of what I've started."

Lil Will shook his head with a look of disgust on his face for his oldest brother. "Nah, nigga. I'm gonna deal with

Chapter Seven

Mark had been summoned back to the estate by Demetri. They, along with Thaddeus, sat in the study talking politics, economics, and finances. He noticed Demetri kept looking at his watch like he was expecting something or someone.

As Mark was about to question his actions, she walked in, escorted by two armed women. Demetri and his brother smiled, and both men hugged her.

"What a pleasant surprise!" Demetri exclaimed.

"Nicole, how are you?" his twin brother entered the conversation asking.

"Uncles, I'm great. Just tired of being out and about so much. I'm in need of a vacation," said Nicole.

Thaddeus nodded. "No problem. Meet - "

"Hi, Mark," Nicole said, cutting her uncle's introduction short.

Mark was stunned. She was slender and curvy with the right posture and a pretty face. He noticed the darker tint of her skin, and came to the conclusion she was biracial.

"Yes, but no," Thaddeus said to Nicole. "His name is Brad. Brad, meet our niece, Nicole, the one you're married to."

He grabbed her left hand and placed a gentle kiss on the back of it. "Nice to meet you Nicole."

Nicole smiled. "Hmm, not bad, Brad."

Demetri clasped his hands together. "Okay, now that the formalities are out of the way, let's get down to business. Welcome to our family, Brad. From now on, you'll no longer be handling such small matters."

Mark nodded. "Thank you, and I accept your welcoming, but who's going to take care of the business for Lil Will?"

Demetri shrugged his shoulders in an "I don't know or care" way. "That's why you've earned a seat at our table, Brad. You're loyal. Don't trouble yourself with something that's already been worked out."

"Okay, Uncle, but what's my new assignment?" Mark asked.

"Enjoying the fruits of your labor," Thaddeus interjected. "I propose a toast: to great health, long life, prosperity, and matrimony. Cheers."

Everyone raised their champagne glasses in salute.

Mark was still confused about his new role, but the confusion came to an end upon hearing Nicole.

"Due to the fact everyone think we're already married in the States, I don't think we should have a wedding here. Prepare to fly out tonight. We're going to Italy."

He looked dumbfounded. Here it was, everything he could possibly want in life coming true.

Demetri and Thaddeus peeped his lost for words expression and had to laugh.

"Brad, did you hear me?" she asked. "Unless you don't want to marry me in reality."

He snapped out of his inner world. "Huh? What did you say?"

Thaddeus couldn't help himself. He burst into uncontrollable laughter, which gave his brother the right to loosen up too. Nicole, on the other hand, was more amused by the reaction she caused to come from him.

"Pack up a few things. We're going to get married in Italy – that is, if you really would like this marriage to be official, and not just a cover story," Nicole said, becoming irritated.

Mark nodded. "Yes, I'm going to pack now. When will we be leaving?"

"As soon as you're done packing," she replied.

He excused himself politely, leaving the others to their laughter.

Demetri smiled at his niece.

"Well, Nicole, marrying him changes things for you."

She looked at her uncle. "Just make sure I get my wedding gifts from both of you, or we're going to have it out."

Both men ceased laughing. Their niece was a woman of many talent, highly trained in Ninjitsu and several other assassin arts, so they didn't know whether to take her serious or to be joking.

Demetri grunted as if to clear his throat. "What would you like for wedding gifts? I'm more than positive we'll be able to provide whatever it is. Right, Thaddeus?"

Thaddeus nodded.

She laughed and hugged them affectionately. "Don't take matters so seriously all the time. I have a sense of humor."

Demetri chuckled. "Yes, but tell that to those who are no longer able to laugh or cry."

"Aw, Uncle Demetri, that's not fair. Anyway, surprise us. What do newlyweds need the most?" Nicole said.

"In your case, nothing. But we'll add more wealth to the wealthy," Thaddeus interjected.

Mark came strolling back into the study, pulling a luggage tower. Everyone looked at him and burst into laughter.

"I guess the jokes on me," said Mark.

"Nephew, you got a real trooper here. Whatever you do, never say no," warned Demetri.

He looked into her eyes, where there was fierceness, compassion, and much more. "Thanks for the warning, but I don't think it's possible for me to say no to such a woman," replied Mark.

Thaddeus slapped the top of the table. "Yep! A match made in Heaven! You two hurry along and return shortly. We shall feast to celebrate such a wonderful union. Go now."

They left in the waiting helicopter.

Demetri and Thaddeus watched from the window.

"Exactly why is it you think she wants to marry him?" Thaddeus asked his brother.

"Well, would you have married someone who didn't share an understanding of the life you live? Besides, they went to college together," replied Demetri.

Thaddeus nodded approvingly. "Thanks for that little bit of information. That explains her knowing his name, because everyone else's name she knows outside of family was targets."

Demetri laughed. "Well, he almost made himself a personal target of hers in college. She liked him back then, but she didn't care for his whorish ways, so to speak."

Thaddeus laughed. "Understood. I think I'll retire on that one for the day."

"Me too," Demetri agreed. "After I arrange for their wedding gifts to greet them on their return. Don't worry brother, I'll take care of yours too while I'm at it."

***

Henry, Mike, Teddy, and Lil Will ended up at Henry's place after the funeral. Lil Will kept eyeing the old school brother who sat in the corner busy on the computer. He knew he was watching him, but was too caught up with completing the task at hand to address him.

"Got it," T said.

T looked up and straight into his eyes. "Lil Willie James, you act like you don't know who I am."

Lil Will looked at him curiously. "Refresh my memory."

T chuckled. "Gangsta, I used to run with y'all niggas' pops. Ain't too long got outta the pen myself."

With that being said, the recognition hit Lil Will. "Well, I'll be a monkey's uncle. T?"

"You called it. Come show an OG some love," T said as he stood. They pounded up and hugged.

"Man, it's good to see ya," said Lil Will.

"Yeah, I say the same. But let's get down to business. You ain't come outta hiding to have a family reunion," said T.

"Definitely didn't, my nigga. All I wanna know are the names and addresses, and I'll personally retire all them fools who had something to do with Bee's death," Lil Will said demandingly.

"Young G, I'm with ya. The rest of 'em can keep the biz straight while we go ring a few doorbells and check a few clowns into the cemetery," T replied.

"It is what it is, fam," said Lil Will.

They sat talking strategy while Teddy, Mike, and Henry talked money and product. By the time night came, everybody knew what their future held: money and murder.

On the way out, Lil Will jumped on the phone. It rang three times before she picked up. "Machumu speaking. Hello," she answered.

"What's up, luv," Lil Will said, putting a little flavor in his voice.

"Boy, I almost didn't answer the phone," Machumu replied.

He laughed. "Almost doesn't count. Anyway, what you doing tonight?"

She sucked her teeth. "Nigga, you asked the question like you 'round the corner."

"Ya never know," Lil Will said, sounding mysterious, "so entertain me. What would you like to do if I showed up at ya front door in a few minutes?"

"I don't fantasize, man. If you showed up, we would find out. Until then, I'm keeping fantasy out the picture," she shot back.

A knock came at the front door.

"Who's knocking on ya door this time of the night," Lil Will asked.

"The hell if I know," she said comically.

"Ain't you going to answer it?" he asked her.

"Hold on," Machumu said.

She walked to the front door and opened it. Immediately, she hung up and threw the phone over on the loveseat.

Lil Will hung up and put his phone in his pocket. "No need to fantasize." He walked in and began tonguing her down.

"I've been thinking about you and this moment so much, baby," she said in between kisses.

"So have I," Lil Will stated in agreement.

They kissed and stripped, leaving a trail of clothes that led to the king-sized bed.

They continued to kiss while exploring each other's bodies with their hands. When he touched between her thighs, she moaned and sighed.

"Make love to me, baby. I want this night to last forever."

His lips left hers and descended to her breasts. He teasingly bit her hard and long nipples while massaging her soft breasts. It was like her heartbeat was in his hands and lips. Without breaking stride, he continued to kiss lower and lower until he reached her sex.

"Oh baby…mmm…baby," Machumu moaned softly.

She moaned and worked her hips to the motion of his tongue slipping in and out and licking up and down between her thighs. Every time he thrust his tongue deep inside of her, he sucked on her clitoris with a hungry passion, causing her body to flex. She grabbed the back of his head, forcing his tongue as far as his face would allow it to reach inside, and grinded out an explosive release.

"Damn, girl, you taste every bit of how I imagined," Lil Will commented while giving her face.

He kissed his way back up to her lips. She opened her legs wider for him to enter her before wrapping her legs around his waist, pulling him fully inside. She gasped as his length filled her up inside. In between kisses, she moaned, enjoying the way he felt inside of her.

They slow grinded to the rhythm of their breath and heartbeat. Her body tensed every time an orgasm claimed her, and his readiness to let go came closer and closer with the warm feeling of her juices flowing around him. Instead of breaking stride, he continued to grind with the motion of her body. She noticed his breathing changed and unwrapped her legs and spread them wide.

"Fill me up, baby. Give me all your love inside of me. Yes. Baby. Mmm. Yes," Machumu moaned softly into his right ear.

His release flowed smoothly. Never had he experienced such a stimulating release before. She kept working her hips, milking him dry. All he could do was close his eyes and enjoy the sensational feeling.

"Not bad, Mr. James. I can imagine waking up and laying down next to you and making love to you for a lifetime," she said seriously.

He nodded, catching his breath. "I was just thinking the same thing." He kissed her lips.

They talked the rest of the night away. He explained to her why he was back in Albany despite being a wanted man. She expressed her understanding, and also let him know he had her full support and that she would help him any way she could.

They made love in between conversation. Finally, at about two-thirty in the morning, they went to sleep with her on top.

***

The woman had return to the agency and made her way to the evidence room. She read through the login catalogue until she found the entry she was looking for. She walked over to the file cabinet and retrieved three files and a several bags containing evidence, and then walked out.

She drove down to the docks and hopped out with the files and evidence. Just as she checked the time, a tall figure dressed in dark clothing carrying a briefcase stepped to the edge of the shadows of a tree.

"Tamika," the figure in the shadows said.

The woman approached the shadows and exchanged the files and evidence for the briefcase.

"It's a nice night out," Tamika said, looking at the moon.

The man nodded. "Yes, it is. Let's hope the day is as nice."

The tall figure stepped back into the darkness. He watched until the woman was safely back in her car and had drove off before disappearing.

***

"Yo, what's good, Dink? Ya ass been on the low lately," said his partner.

Dink pounded up his right hand man. "Yeah, man. Family issues."

His partner's expression changed. "Yeah, I heard 'bout yo' brotha. That was some ill shit. Hold on a minute."

As he stepped inside, Dink sat on the front porch in deep thought. His greed had cost him his brother and, the way it looked, his family.

"Never again," Dink thought out loud.

"What's that, fam?" his right hand man asked, thinking he was talking to him.

Dink shook his head. "Shit. Just talking to God, my nigga. What ya got for me?"

His runner sat the duffle bag down in between them on the porch. "Everything plus the go-back."

"That's what's up. I'll see what I can cop from some outta town niggas later on and swing back through," Dink said as he grabbed the duffle bag.

He jumped up to leave, but as soon as he stepped off the porch, bullets started flying his way. He ducked and caught grip running behind the house. Whoever had shot at him didn't give chase, but drove off in a hurry. With gun in hand, he crept cautiously back to the front through the back door, and the first thing he spotted was that his right hand man had been hit in the leg.

Dink put his gun on the chair and checked on his partner. "You a'ight, fam?"

He nodded. "Yeah, I'm good. I'll hit my baby mama up to help me. She's a registered nurse. My nigga, you be safe."

Dink picked up the duffle bag and left.

***

Lil Will woke up to breakfast in bed. It had been a while since he had a home cooked meal, and it showed. He wolfed down the salmon patties, homemade biscuits, apple jam and eggs. He didn't give any thought to the orange juice.

"So, this is how it's going down at yo' spot," he said to Machumu approvingly. "I gotta stop by two to three times a day."

She laughed. "For what, when you got me at home?"

He shrugged his shoulders, smiling. "Maybe to catch you on break, and eat me a happy meal."

Her eyes lit up with surprise. "Oh, so that's what I am?"

Lil Will shook his head. "No, that's how ya taste make me feel."

She smiled and she was about to respond when someone knocked on the back door.

At first she thought she was mishearing where the knock was coming from until they knocked again, using a certain rhythm. She jumped off the edge of the bed and ran to the back door.

She opened the door to see a tall figure standing there with a backpack draped across the shoulder. She stepped out onto the porch and eased the door closed behind her.

"How may I help you this morning?" Machumu asked the man.

"Tamika," he replied. "It's going to be a sunny day."

Machumu nodded. "So the weatherman says."

"Yes, and they also sent this thermometer as a gift to gauge the heat." The tall figure handed her the backpack.

She didn't even bother looking in it. "Thank you for the early morning news. Have a great day."

"So shall we all," he stated.

The tall figure walked off and disappeared in the woods.

She waited a few minutes before going back inside. Back in the house, she quickly ducked off into the washroom and opened the backpack. Inside there were three files and several bags containing evidence, which brought a smile to her face. Quickly, she put it back in and stashed the backpack in a secret compartment behind the washer, and then ran back to the bedroom. She jumped on top of him and began kissing him passionately.

"Mmm. What's the occasion?" Lil Will said in between kisses.

Machumu smiled seductively. "Happiness. Just go with the flow."

They made love again. She took him for the ride of his life. On top, she worked her hips, and the muscles between her thighs popped hard and fast. All he could do was grab her shoulders and thrust up as she came down.

"Oh my God! Mmm...mmm!" she moaned and screamed.

Lil Will thrust up inside of her. "Hell yeah! Ride this dick, girl! Ride this! Oh shit!" Before he could catch himself, he came inside of her.

Feeling his release inside of her, she popped faster and harder until her juices flowed and mixed with his inside.

"Mmm...baby..." she moaned while she rocked back and forth on top until the sensation traveling through her calmed.

Quickly, Machumu jumped up, ran to the bathroom, and took a shower. Once she finished, she walked back into the bedroom while getting dressed for work. She had intended to tell him something, but only smiled upon seeing him sound asleep.

***

Product sold and money made, Teddy, Henry, and Mike were back at the counting table. Everything was definitely everything. They didn't come up short, but way over the go-back price. Everybody put five thousand to the side for Dee and her son.

Once the counting was over and the money placed in briefcases, Teddy had them help carry it out to his car and put it in the trunk. He asked T to take the fifteen thousand to Dee before jumping in his ride and driving off. At the stop sign, he called his connect, who finally answered on the fourth try.

"Yeah. What's good?" his connect answered.

Teddy watched the flow of traffic. "Great day out on the lake. Caught more fish than I had bait."

"Alright, bro. Let me see what I can do for you. Right now, I'm on my way outta the country. I'll hit you back in a minute with details," he said.

"Bet. One, fam," replied Teddy.

They hung up.

His connect dialed another number that was answered immediately.

"Didn't I tell you not to worry about that, Brad? What's his number?" the man answered, frustrated.

He gave him Teddy's number. Without responding, the line went dead.

As he was about to call Teddy back, Nicole grabbed the phone, dropped it on the deck of the helicopter, and stomped it.

"No business on this trip, Brad. Besides, that part of your life ended when you decided to get on the helicopter."

Looking into her eyes, seeing the multiple layers of hidden strengths, he grabbed her hands in his and kissed her lips.

"And I made the decision consciously."

Chapter Eight

As Teddy pulled into the driveway, his "Ghetto Dope" ringtone went off. "Hello?"

"Yes, I suggest you change your ringtone. It's very tell, tell," the caller answered.

"Anyway, the same place, however, your contact will address you as Ted. Everything else can remain the same."

"Okay," Teddy replied. "I'm on the way."

"See you soon then," the contact said. The contact on the other end hung up.

Teddy backed out of the driveway and back into traffic. Switching lanes, he got off on the next exit. He was determined to keep things running smoothly and stay away from the drama in the streets.

On that note, he took the man's advice, and deleted his ringtones.

Five hours later, he pulled in at the meeting place. He hopped out and smoothed over his business attire before strolling inside. He spoke to passing couples and singles on their way out. As he sat at the usual table away from the window, a baldheaded middle-aged man approached and sat across from him.

"Lovely day out, Ted," the man said.

Ted nodded. "That it is. Considered taking the youngsters out on the lake, but realized I was out of bait. Imagine that."

The contact chuckled. "Well, let's see about getting you that bait, buddy. Come on."

They left, chatting like they'd been friends for years. Teddy tailed him down to the docks, where the exchange took place.

"The whale is a couple days out from you," the contact informed him.

"One day I'm going to catch the whale and leave regular fishing alone," Teddy said confidently.

The contact looked at him serious. "I'll be sure to keep that in mind, Ted."

They shook hands and went their separate ways.

***

Sopia and Sabrina were at her apartment when Mike and Henry showed up. They kicked it strong, blazing an ounce of some gas and sipping Bacardi 151 mixed with Southern Comfort. Mike brought up the fact that Lil Will was in Albany just to see how she would react.

How did she react? She pulled his sex out and sucked him until he came and swallowed every drop.

Without saying a word, she walked upstairs and brushed her teeth. As she gargled and spit, he pulled up behind her, lifted the skirt and pulled the panties to the side, and started long stroking her from the back slow. She moaned and threw it back on him.

"Mmm, daddy...don't play with this pussy," Sopia moaned, enjoying the moment.

Mike changed the tempo from slow to hard and fast. "That's how you want it? That's how you like it?"

"Yeah! Yeah!" she screamed.

Sopia was sloppy wet between her thighs. He felt like he had entered a good hot bath. Before he knew it, he was exploding inside of her.

She continued to moan lustfully. "Yes, baby, cum... Let it all out inside of this good pussy."

He grabbed her hips and short stroked hard and fast until he came again inside of her. Feeling her own release coming, she grinded back up on him until it flowed around him. Afterwards, they jumped in the shower together.

When they returned downstairs, Sabrina and Henry were going at it hard on the couch. He had her folded up like a pretzel, pounding away. She looked over his shoulder. Seeing them, she smiled with the sexiest sex face.

"Roll some more blunts or something! Y'all act like y'all ain't never seen a bitch get gutted! Yeah! Just like that! Give me that dick! Yeah nigga!"

Mike and Sopia started twisting blunts. When their partners were finished sexing each other crazy, they smoked and drank some more while kicking the shit.

***

When Lil Will got out of bed, the day was halfway over. *Damn, she put it on me*, he thought. He got dressed and made his way over to Henry's crib, where he and T sat for a minute smoking a blunt of Purp. T filled him in on the whereabouts of the crew that had actually called the hit.

"A'ight, my nigga, you ready?" T asked Lil Will.

Lil Will nodded. "Let's get to it, OG."

T brought out the arsenal. "Pick ya tools, Lil Willie."

He grabbed an SKS with two extra clips and two nines.

T nodded approvingly. "Nice choice. Let's ride."

They hopped in a dark blue Caprice Classic with tinted windows. They rolled over to the Westside and cruised the blocks. It was a normal day. Youngsters hustling and li'l fast hot in the ass teenage girls out to fuck for a check and pleasure.

As they drove around to the back side of the projects, T spotted a familiar face. He scrolled through his messages until he found the one he was looking for and opened it. He looked through the face shots and looked back at the men who were trapping at the courts. All positive identification.

"Young G, today is our lucky day," T told Lil Will. "There all them fools are right there. I'm gonna drive down near the woods and let you out so we can catch 'em slipping."

He drove on around and Lil Will jumped out and ran into the woods. He knew the area, so creeping up on them wasn't so hard. He watched from behind a tree when T pulled up and rolled the window down halfway and one of the guys strolled over.

"What up, my nigga? I got the works. What cha need?"

"Yo' life, nigga." T put a slug between his eyes.

Upon seeing the man fall, Lil Will emerged from the woods, chopping the others down with the SKS. They tried to run, but it was an open field.

"Where y'all niggas think ya going? Don't run now, fuck niggas!" T yelled, opening the car door.

T jumped out the car and upped the AK-47. He and Lil Will end up meeting in the middle of the basketball court with seven dead bodies.

T looked around them. "Well, that's that. Let's ride, fam."

They trotted back to the car and peeled out. T deleted the facial shots of the dead men. There were still nine more left. As they were about to pull up on the scene, Lil Will's phone rang.

He answered and said, "I'm in the middle of something right now. Can you call me back?"

"Lil Will," he said, "this isn't a callback call. Besides, how is it that the head of the table is jeopardizing his legacy with something his crew can handle? Not a smart move."

Lil Will automatically recognized the voice. "It's been a while. What's going on?"

"You must return to your duties," he demanded.

Lil Will laughed. "That's kind of hard with a manhunt on my head."

He sighed. "Was on your head. But keep doing what you're doing, and there will probably be one on you that won't come off so easily."

Lil Will's expression became serious. "So, I'm a free man?"

The caller didn't waste time responding. "Go to the airport in the morning. Someone will meet you there to fly you over. And bring your girlfriend. Machumu is her name, isn't it?"

It never ceased to amaze him the information the man always had. "Alright, we'll be there."

"Great," he replied. "We'll have a family reunion. Sort of, anyway. Until then, be smart about your business." He hung up.

Lil Will put the phone on the dashboard and sighed. "Say, fam, bust a U. Change of plans."

He turned around.

Lil Will picked up the phone and called Mike.

Mike answered on the second ring. "What up, fam?"

"Henry with ya?" Lil Will asked.

"Yeah," Mike said. "We over at Sopia's crib. Why, what's going on?"

"Y'all sit tight. I'm on the way over," Lil Will said.

"A'ight," Mike replied.

They hung up.

Ten minutes later, T and Lil Will pulled into the apartments and hopped out. Sopia opened the door and let them in.

Lil Will looked her up and down. "What's up, Sopia? You doing alright?"

She nodded. "Couldn't be better." Sopia yelled over her shoulder and said, "Mike, Henry, Lil Will, and T here!" She looked back at Lil Will. "Come on in."

They walked into the living room, where Henry and Mike sat with Sabrina smoking. Sopia sat back on Mike's lap.

"Is everything good, fam?" Mike asked Lil Will.

Lil Will nodded. "Hell yeah, Mike. I just got a call that I gotta handle. Me and Machumu 'bout to be outta town for a minute."

"So, what you need us to do?" he asked.

"Y'all keep handling shit accordingly. Everything else is already lined up to get done. Sabrina and Sopia, I know y'all can fuck some shit up in a kitchen, so I need y'all to fill in at the restaurant 'til we get back. Are we good?" Lil Will said.

Sabrina and Sopia nodded. "Yeah, we good."

"Bet," he replied.

Lil Will and T left.

Sabrina looked at Sopia and smiled. "Homegirl, we just got employed."

They burst into laughter. Mike rubbed Sopia on the thigh. It was a relief to know his partner wasn't tripping over a piece of pussy.

***

Mark and Nicole made it to Italy. He hadn't ever been there, but being there definitely made him want to come back again when the opportunity came. Seeing his approving expression, she smiled.

"I'm glad you like the scenery. We can live the rest of our lives here."

Mark smiled back. "Sounds like a plan to me. I mean, when you're ready to retire from your profession."

Nicole shook her head and laughed. "Come on, Brad. Let's get settled in."

The two armed women grabbed their luggage. Mark followed Nicole to the waiting car, which he could tell was armored, with three more armed women bodyguards. When they were in and on their way, he allowed his curiosity to get the best of him. "Are all your personal staff women?"

She nodded proudly. "The majority are. Is there something wrong with women being bodyguards?"

"Not at all," he replied quickly.

"Good, because I was going to ask you to challenge either one of them to a friendly spar. I guarantee you'd change your way of thinking after the fact," Nicole stated seriously.

He shook his head, surrendering. "I'll take your word for it."

She giggled. "You always were a smart man. Whorish, but smart."

Mark eyed her closely. "You talk like we know each other."

Nicole smirked. "No need to bring back memories. We'll save that for our honeymoon."

The rest of the ride was silent. They pulled up at an estate on the outskirts. He observed the guards at the gates go about doing a security check on the vehicles. Ten minutes later, they were walking inside.

"Welcome to my humble home. I'm more than sure you'll find everything here to your liking," she told him.

One of the chefs walked up to her, speaking Italian. She hugged the short lady while responding in Italian. She looked back at him and said, "Dinner - "

"Will be served in forty minutes," he interjected. "I took Italian for a third language."

She looked surprised. "Aren't you full of surprises? Let's wash up for dinner."

Nicole showed him to a guest room, which had a full bath inside. She told him he would be sleeping there until after they were married. He didn't object. Not that it would've changed her mind if he had.

After the maid put his things neatly into dresser drawers and the walk-in closet and left, he jumped in the shower. Even the water felt different on his skin. He dried off and got dressed. While he was putting on his Stacy Adams suit, a maid came in and told him he'd been summoned to dine with the mistress of the house.

The way the maid titled her caused him to smile inside and out. She escorted him to the dining room, which should've been called a dining hall. The room was big enough to hold a banquet plus. He realized they weren't dining alone.

Upon entering, everyone stood. Nicole was standing off to the side with her usual serious demeanor. She reached a hand out towards him, and he walked over and embraced it with his and kissed it.

"Mother, father, sisters, brother and friends, meet my fiancé, Mark Thames."

Everyone spoke. Her mother and sisters greeted him with a kiss on the cheek, and her father and brother gave him a firm handshake and grip on the shoulder. They all returned to their seats, and the food was served.

Once the table was set and the family was served, the chefs and maids came in and dined with them.

They chatted and laughed until everyone was full and satisfied. The maids started cleaning the table of dishes and food. How they were doing it was confusing to Mark, and it made Nicole laugh.

"Food doesn't get thrown away here. What's left over is taken to those who are less fortunate," she explained.

That warmed his heart. Here she was, an expert killing machine with a heart of gold. What more could he ask for, he thought to himself. They retired to their rooms for the night after she told him their wedding would be held in two days.

***

Lil Will and Machumu arrived at the airport at 7:33 a.m. He thought he was going to have a hard time talking her into taking the trip with him, but it was the exact opposite. She was happy and excited about the whole ordeal. He watched the private jet land and come to a stop.

"Looks like our ride just arrived. Come on," he said.

They hopped out with their luggage in tow. The door opened and stairs unfolded as they approached. A man wearing a beige three-piece suit stepped into the doorway, smiling.

"It's good to see you alive, Lil Will. And how're you doing, young lady?"

Machumu smiled. "I'm fine."

"Good. Let's get back in the air," he said.

Lil Will and Machumu stepped aboard. After refueling, they were airborne. Three hours later, they touched down in Texas, where a car awaited them that drove them straight to the estate.

Demetri met them at the door. "What a pleasant surprise! How've you been?"

"On the run," Lil Will said dully.

"Not you," Demetri stated. "I'm talking to her."

Machumu walked up to him, and they hugged.

"I've been great, Demetri."

Lil Will was dumbfounded. All this time he thought she was some down-to-earth sister with great family values.

It tickled Demetri to see his facial expression.

"Young man, you have a lot to learn about the lifestyle you're in. Anyhow, come on in. Other guests are waiting on us."

Lil Will couldn't get his mind off of the newfound information. She just looked at him and shrugged her shoulders.

"You never asked."

They followed Demetri into the meeting room, where several people sat entertaining each other in conversation. Some of them Lil Will remembered from the last meeting he'd attended. Others, he didn't know, but Machumu seemed to know everyone present. And it didn't take long for him to learn why.

"Daddy! Auntie Sarah! Sis," Machumu said happily. She didn't know who she wanted to hug first.

Thaddeus, Demetri, and Mr. Cobb stood off to the side, enjoying the scene. After they had hugged, asked of each other's health, and hugged again, everyone settled down and waited on the food to be served. While waiting, Demetri took the floor.

"Ladies and gentlemen, family and friends, it's a beautiful day. But I didn't call you here to discuss the weather. This meeting is to remind everyone of my decision to hand this business over to Lil Will. With that being said, we will not discuss business during the rest of this evening."

He sat down. Everyone looked in Lil Will's direction. He was still mulling over how deeply involved his girl was in the mob life. She squeezed his hand and brought him back to reality. He stood and took the floor.

"Good evening, ladies and gentlemen. I know the past few months have been shaky. I know they have been for me. But I assure you that the heat coming from the south will die down soon."

"What makes you so sure?" asked Sarah.

He wasn't ready for the question, especially not coming from Machumu's Aunt Sarah.

"Because what's happening right now down south is related to the death of my youngest brother. Another crew killed him for some foolishness our oldest brother did. That's why I'm so sure," Lil Will stated.

"So you think vengeance is best sought by physically killing them?" asked Sarah.

"They killed my brother, and I'm killing their whole crew," Lil Will said coldly.

Sarah looked at her niece questioningly. Demetri could see the turn of events coming and intervened.

"Surely he has much to learn about the business he's pledged his life to. Assets are assets for a reason. Still, vengeance is only sweet when you can enjoy the taste of victory without consequence. Now please, enjoy the meal."

Lil Will sat back down next to Machumu. He quickly realized he'd taken a step above his league. Her family members were very important government figures, and he was only a street king. They ate and he listened silently to the conversations about him.

After the dinner, Thaddeus had informed everyone that they were their guests for the remainder of the night and to pick whatever guest rooms they wanted to be their sleeping quarters. On the way to theirs, they talked.

"Listen Willie. If you gonna play the game, learn the rules of game and the rules the rest of the players play by. That's the only way to last in this world, and the only way to gain the respect of it," Machumu advised Lil Will.

Lil Will was still stuck on how much he didn't know about Machumu. "You can say that again. Here I am thinking you just a good housewife only to find out you a daughter of the mob itself."

Her smile faded into a serious expression. "Consider yourself lucky, baby."

They made love and retired for the night holding each other.

Chapter Nine

T had rounded up the S.M.F. crew. They sat on the Southside kicking it when Dink pulled up and jumped out. Everybody pounded him up.

T eyed him closely. "What up, Dink?"

"I'm riding with y'all, T. A nigga got to start righting his wrongs somewhere," Dink replied.

T nodded, feeling what Dink had said. "Words of a real G, my nigga. Let's do this. We ain't taking any prisoners. We hitting these Westside niggas hard and fast."

They mounted up and rode out.

Instead of driving through the projects, they pulled onto a dirt road walking distance away and hopped out strapped. It was night, so T had them all dressed in black and masked up. Like a real live military unit they crept through the woods, and when the night lights became visible, he brought them to a halt. In a whisper tone he gave them final instructions, mostly not to waste a surprise attack missing bodies, and also to make every slug count as if their depended on it.

T cocked his gun. "A'ight, let's get it."

Dink was the first out the woods dumping, catching two of them in the chest. T used his timing to shoot the street lights out.

"Go! Go!" T yelled.

Everybody emerged from the woods busting their guns.

Nobody on the Westside was prepared for the war they brought to their doorstep. One of the men was on the run, but Dink was on him. As he grabbed the doorknob of the apartment door, Dink pumped three slugs in his back, causing him to fall through the door dead.

He ran back to where the rest of the crew was handling business.

Everybody Dink passed, he put a slug in their heads just to make sure they were dead. With no Westside hustler left standing, they dipped back the same way them came.

***

Teddy was down at the docks with the shipment. After the boatman had sailed off, he called Mike and Henry, who showed up shortly afterwards. They loaded the product into their cars and drove to the warehouse, where they broke it down three ways and called their crews to come pick it up for distribution.

As they were getting ready to leave, Henry's phone rang. He looked at the caller's ID and saw that it was T.

Henry answered his phone. "What's up, fam?"

"We don' deadened that shit, Lil Henry," T said with excitement in his voice.

"That's the move. Maybe the streets will get a li'l quiet so this money can be made," Henry replied.

"Where y'all headed?" asked T.

"Back to my crib. What's up?" he asked T.

"I'm on the way. I got a fool-ass plan," said T.

Henry nodded. "A'ight. One, fam." He hung up.

"Teddy, that was T," stated Henry.

Teddy looked up from what he was doing. "Yeah? What's good?"

Henry shook his head and laughed. "A whole lot of dead Westside niggas."

Teddy nodded. "Understood."

"Yep. T said he's on his way to the crib. Says he got a plan," Henry said.

"Shit, let's go hear him out," replied Teddy.

They left the warehouse and arrived at Henry's spot. Henry, Mike, and Teddy walked in to find T sitting in front of the computer typing with a blunt hanging from his mouth.

Knowing they were there, he stopped typing, took a deep pull on the blunt, and passed it to Teddy.

"So, y'all niggas ready to hear this shit?" T asked, excited. They sat down and got in rotation on the green.

"We 'bout to monopolize this shit," T said. "I'm going to personally go 'round and start a peace treaty talk. Whoever's down with the movement, we supply. That way we move more weight in a lesser timeframe."

"Not a bad idea, but the shit is gonna cut down our profit," Teddy reminded T.

"Teddy, my nigga, we ain't gonna give these fools uncut shit. We stepping on shit twice. If we get a thousand bricks, we turn that thousand into three thousand, and charge a thousand less a brick," T responded.

Teddy nodded. "Now I see ya figures, fam. A'ight, we on that the next shipment."

"One more thing," T said while hitting the blunt. "That nigga Dink did his thang."

Teddy was curious. "What you talking 'bout?"

T explained how Dink showed up right before they mobbed over on the Westside, how he was the first one to pop off and everything. The others had a new profound respect for him, however, they weren't ready to let him fully in on the move. They agreed to take a vote when Lil Will got back, or if he didn't come back, to vote in his absence.

***

Two days flew by for Mark. There was a lot of shopping, being tailored for a wedding suit and checking out wedding scenes and bands, all the things he didn't see himself doing so soon, but here he was about to tie the knot.

Nicole had liked the view of the prairie top, so that's where they stood holding hands, surrounded by her family and friends. Like Demetri and Thaddeus, she was an atheist, so there was no preacher, rabbi, or priest to join them in matrimony. They exchanged vows, kissed, and jumped over the broom and crushed two wineglasses upon landing on the other side.

Nicole was all smiles and excitement. "Wow! I can't believe this has happened! Do you know how long I've waited for this moment?"

He looked at her puzzled. "How long?"

She laughed, surprised. "Since we were in college boy!"

He paused and eyed her closely. Finally, his memory kicked in, and he laughed while picking her up spinning around. "Patrice? Oops. Nicole?"

She kissed him on the lips. "Yep!"

They had the most elegant dinner ever – at least, that's what one of the chefs explained to Mark. Whether it was to make him feel special or at home didn't make a difference to him because being with her already brought that affect.

They danced, and he ended up dancing with her mother while she danced with her father.

When they returned to the estate, everyone left them alone. As they stepped into the bedroom, he noticed the bed canopy draped with emerald green silk draping. Nicole undressed before him, staring into his eyes.

Seeing the passion, Mark did the same before picking her up and carrying her over to the bed.

They kissed for a while. As he reached between her thighs, she stopped him and sat up.

He ceased in his advances. "What's wrong?"

Nicole was nervous. "Mark, I'm a virgin. Try to understand what I'm saying."

He stared into her eyes. "I'll understand death for you. Relax, luv. I promise you I won't hurt you."

She leaned into his kisses as he eased her back down. With much skill, he explored every portion of her body with his lips. Between her thighs, he sexed her with his tongue until she came. The passion and delicate touch of his tongue was driving her crazy.

She moaned and squirmed, wanting to run away from the pleasure, but her mind fought to stay within its bounds. Before she knew it, she was rubbing all over his head and moving her hips with the motion of his tongue.

"Oh, Mark. Oh baby," Nicole moaned uncontrollably.

She came again and again.

Seeing she'd loosened up, he kissed his way back up to her breasts and took his time sucking on them both. He entered her slowly, causing her to moan and whimper. Once fully inside, he didn't move, but continued to kiss her sweet-tasting lips.

"I want you so bad, Nicole. Mmm..." said Mark.

He stroked her slowly, about a fifteen second lapse between each stroke. The pleasure outweighed the pain. He kissed the tears that came from her eyes. Her tightness and virgin wetness caused him to release quickly inside of her.

He laid on the bed beside her mind in a world of wonder. She rolled over on her side to face him, and they kissed until they fell asleep holding hands, their bodies in the shape of a heart.

***

Lil Will and Machumu were back in Albany. According to the report he got, everything had been going smoothly. The shipment was in and being sold, Sabrina and Sopia had kept their word, and The South Side Mafia Family had taken it to the Westside. What really threw him for a loop was Dink's involvement with the gunplay.

That gave him a lot to consider. On their way home, they stopped by his mother's house. She met them at the front door and hugged her son.

"Hey, baby. How's my son doing? And who's this young lady you got with you?"

"Mama, I'm okay. This is my future wife, Machumu. Machumu, this is my mother, Mrs. Ruby," Lil Will said, introducing the two women.

They hugged.

They walked inside and had a long sit down talk with his mother. She had so many stories to tell Machumu about the man she was in love with. And at the end of every story, she realized why she was so in love with him.

Lil Will looked at the time. "Well, Mama, it's getting late, and we've had a long flight."

"Okay, baby. Y'all take care, and come back to see Mama whenever you out and about," his mother said.

"Alright, Mama," he replied.

They all hugged before Lil Will and Machumu hopped in the car and drove off.

"I really like your mama. She's down to earth," Machumu said.

Lil Will nodded in agreement. "Yeah, the same I thought about you 'til a couple days ago."

Machumu got defensive. "And what is that supposed to mean?"

Lil Will shook his head. "Nothing, other than you ain't the everyday average woman."

She laughed. "I thought you knew that when you met me. Oh, I forgot, you were looking at me with the wrong eye attached to the wrong head."

They came to a red light.

He chuckled. "You got me there. I'm glad we met."

Machumu smiled. "Did you mean what you said at your mama's house?"

"If I said it," said Lil Will, "I meant it. I ain't an Indian giver in word or gifts, Machumu."

"I'm definitely going to hold ya to it," she replied.

A car pulled up beside them at the red light. She looked over at the driver, who seemed fidgety. Something wasn't right.

"Baby, are you strapped?" she asked Lil Will.

He glanced at her out of the corner of his right eye. "Why, what's up?"

"Give me your gun," Machumu demanded.

Lil Will frowned. "What? What's up, Machumu?"

She was getting irritated with him. "Nigga, just hand me the fucking gun! Now!"

He handed her the gun. She cocked the nine and held it behind her back as she jumped out of the car.

Lil Will was paranoid. "Machumu, what the fuck are you doing?"

He soon found out.

Machumu propped herself up against the car beside them at the red light. "Hey, boo. What you niggas up to tonight?"

The driver grinned. "Miss Lady, get that nigga you riding with to pull 'round da corna."

Exactly what she thought. Machumu looked to make sure no one was in the backseat, and without hesitation, she upped the nine and emptied the clip in the driver and passenger. His foot came off the brakes and the car started rolling through the intersection. She jumped back in like nothing had happened. Lil Will was stunned for a minute.

"Come back to earth, baby. Drive," she said.

He took off. She had to make him slow down.

He was nervous. "What the hell was that about?"

Now she was really irritated. "Nigga, your life! Those niggas wanted me to trick yo' ass around the corner so they could end yo' life! That's what's wrong with y'all street niggas! Y'all don't pay attention to shit!"

And she was right, Lil Will thought to himself. "I'm sorry, Machumu."

She was upset. "I don't want to hear that shit! Just drive!"

He didn't attempt to argue. Seeing she didn't mind putting a slug in a nigga got his mind right. He had a real trooper.

She hit a number on speed dial. "Hey Uncle Daquan. Yeah, I'm fine. Just had a little incident to take place at an intersection. Okay. Thank you and love you." She hung up the phone.

Lil Will wasn't sure of what to say, so he just kept quiet. He thought about his right hand man Mark and tried to hit him up, but the phone kept sending him to voicemail. He called Demetri to see if he had any idea where he might be.

"You mean my nephew Brad," Demetri corrected him. "He's out of the country at the moment."

Lil Will was confused. "Then who's running the show?"

"Everyone is counting on you to. Besides, he's no longer involved in this lifestyle," Demetri said.

Lil Will sighed with relief. "That's what's up. I was just making sure he's good."

"He's awesome! They'll be back in the States soon. I'll make sure to send you an invitation to the party. Until then, keep business business," Demetri stated.

He hung up the phone.

Lil Will looked at her out of the corner of his eye to see if she showed any sign of nervousness or fear, but there were signs of neither.

She peeped his movement. "Concentrate on what's in front of you. You're driving."

He laughed. "That's not a problem."

Machumu turned sideways in the passenger seat. "Oh, really?"

She leaned over in the seat, took his sex into her hand, and started massaging it. When it hardened, she wrapped her lips around the tip and sucked him while playing with the head with her tongue.

His toes curled up. "Oh shit. Hold up. Damn, baby."

She stopped. "Concentrate, nigga."

She worked him over so good he swerved a couple times. She felt his sex starting to pulsate and stopped before he could cum.

"Pull over right here."

He pulled onto the dirt road, turned the lights off, and killed the ignition. She let his seat all the way back and eased down on top of him. Since he was already on edge, it didn't take too much winding and grinding of her hips for him to explode inside of her.

Breathing hard, he said, "Machumu, I love you."

"I love you too."

She kissed him passionately while grinding out a nut of her own.

Feeling satisfied, she straightened up her dress and sat back in the passenger seat. "Now drive."

***

Agent Harris had met with Special Agent Sarah at her ranch style home on the lake. They sat in beach chairs, sipping wine coolers, looking out on the water.

"Mama, I seen the way you looked at Mu," her daughter stated.

"She should make better decisions sometimes. No need of being with someone you'll spend more time cleaning up behind than learning to love," she replied.

Agent Harris nodded and sipped her drink. "Understood. Who knows? Maybe she'll get him right in the head."

Sarah sighed. "I hope so because if anything happens to her, I won't hesitate to put a bullet in his skull."

Her daughter nodded and held her drink up as to agree. "I was thinking more diabolically, but that'll do."

They shared a laugh.

"So, what's up with you and what's his name?" Sarah asked her daughter.

She smiled. "Who, Damien?"

"Yeah," Sarah said.

"He wants to get married and leave the States," Agent Harris replied.

""nd?" asked her mother.

Sarah's daughter set down her cup. "Mama, I'm not trying to leave you."

Sarah frowned. "Child, please! If you're making good money doing the dirt you're doing now, think about the money you'll make when you're in the family and not just a friend."

She laughed. "I see your point."

"But only if you love him, baby," Sarah added. "Make no mistake in marrying a man like that if you don't plan on staying with him."

Agent Harris gave her a thumbs up. "I got you."

They continued to talk and laugh until it was time to take it in. Both of them had to be at the agency bright and early the next morning.

***

The baldheaded man watched the activity inside the house through the night vision goggles from the tree line. Upon seeing the old white guy chasing after the younger lady playfully inside, he made a call.

"I have the target in sight. He seems to have a friend over for company. Okay. No problem."

He hung up the phone and crept over to the side of the house. He found an open window and eased inside. He could hear the couple, and from the sounds, they had gotten intimate. He pulled the sword out of its sheath.

"Yes, daddy! Yes! Lick this pussy good! Get your money worth, big daddy," he heard.

The guy dressed in the camouflage ninja suit moved swiftly and silent through the house. He entered the dimly lit room at a crawl until he reached the bed, where the man was performing oral sex on the nicely-shaped woman. She had her eyes closed, enjoying the performance. He stood up, and with the first cutting strike of the sword, he cut the man's head off. And before the woman could gather her senses to scream, he slit her throat.

Back out the same window he'd climbed through, he made his way to the car parked on the other side of the tree line. When he got in, he pressed the detonator. The explosives he'd planted around the house the night before brought the house down. He made the call.

"It's done. Okay. Yes, I just received the address. Alright. You too."

He hung up and drove on to the next destination. He parked on the side of the road and moved between the rows of houses like a shadow. Upon reaching the home belonging to his target, he crouched in the shadows. He listened for the sound of any movement and activity inside, but heard none, and quickly found out why.

The patrol car pulled into the driveway and the man got out, still dressed in his uniform. The assassin in the shadows grabbed the hilt of the sword, waiting for the perfect timing. As the deputy opened the trunk of his car and reached in, he emerged like a ghost. Without breaking stride, he thrust the blade through his side, and when he made an attempt to stand, the blade went through his neck smoothly.

The deputy's body collapsed to the ground, but his head fell into the trunk. Back in his car, he called the employer.

"Taken care of. You're welcome. See you soon."

He drove off. As he reached the sign exiting Albany, he grinned.

Chapter Ten

Lil Will woke up, and Machumu was already gone. He turned the television on to the news. At first, he was still hazy, but when the breaking news report flashed across the screen, his eyes opened wide. The pictures of the county mayor, sheriff, and some call girl were posted as deceased.

"The mayor and this young woman's body were found after the fire was finally put out at his home. Like the sheriff, his head had been severed from the rest of his body. Local police and sheriff departments are calling the murders assassinations. We'll have more details at six."

He turned the volume down. He couldn't think of any reason someone would want the mayor and sheriff dead. As his mind turned over and over, the phone vibrated on the nightlight table.

"Hello," Lil Will answered.

"What's good, fam?" Mark said in high spirits.

"Mark," Lil Will said, surprised.

"Brad," Mark corrected him, "but yeah, it's me. How you been holding up?"

"My nigga, shit been real, but a G holding things down," Lil Will replied.

"That's good to hear. Listen, you, your girl, and Teddy gotta fly out to the spot on the next flight. It's already been paid for," said Mark.

"What spot?" asked Lil Will.

"Nigga," Mark began, "the biggest spot you ever been in. I'll see you soon." Mark hung up.

Lil Will was about to call Machumu, but she walked through the door. "I was 'bout to call you."

Machumu had a look of frustration on her face. "You haven't learned anything yet, have you?"

He didn't respond. Instead, he dialed his brother's number. He picked up.

"What's good, bro?" Lil Will said to Teddy.

Teddy took a right turn at the light. "I'm in traffic."

"Where ya headed?" asked Lil Will.

"Nigga, I'm meeting you at the airport," Teddy said, thinking Lil Will would already know. "We'll get up then." Teddy hung up on him.

Lil Will threw the phone on the bed, got up, and started packing. Machumu stood in the doorway to the bedroom laughing.

"Stop trying so hard, baby. This business is self-run. All the head does is keeps the rest of the body safe and functioning. This shit ain't rocket science."

Lil Will stopped packing and looked up at her. "Are you going to pack something?"

She laughed comically. "For what?"

He finished packing and they left.

When they arrived at the airport, Teddy was waiting for them. Lil Will looked his brother over, who was dressed in a tailor-made business suit with the suede shoes to match.

"A'ight, bro! You got ya dress code up to part," Lil Will commented.

Teddy brushed down the front of the coat. "Yeah, I take sound advice from made men."

Machumu laughed. "Something you need to teach your brother how to do."

Teddy started laughing.

They boarded their flight. In so many words, without calling their names, Teddy informed him he'd left Henry and Mike in charge. After the plane touched down and they got off, he gave them the rundown on the plan T was working on.

"That's good thinking. Listen, bro - " Lil Will started to say before Machumu cut him off.

Machumu grunted. Understanding that was his cue to be quiet without her saying it, Lil Will closed his mouth.

The ride to the estate was quiet. Teddy took in the scene with admiration, thinking to himself how one day he would have a spot like it. At the estate, Demetri, Thaddeus, Mark, and Nicole greeted them at the door. Teddy shook hands with everyone.

Machumu hugged Demetri and his brother before shaking hands with the others. Lil Will shook hands with everyone but Mark, who he bear hugged.

"Man, it's been a long time coming," Lil Will said to him.

Mark stepped back beside Nicole. "Yeah, it has. Meet my wife, Nicole."

Lil Will was dumbfounded. "What?"

"His wife," Nicole stated in a serious tone of voice.

Thaddeus noticed the irritation his niece was feeling and interjected.

"Okay everyone. Let's get this party started! Today, we celebrate the matrimony of Brad and Nicole. Tomorrow, we celebrate business management."

Everyone walked in. The maids took their things to the guestrooms while they all went to the banquet hall. The table was already being set. They sat in conversation, waiting on the feast to be served.

Thaddeus and his brother were talking to Teddy. It was a casual conversation to see where his mind was at. So far, he was doing great. Another couple walked in, who Machumu automatically recognized

"Sis and Damien!" Machumu screamed happy.

"Well, well. Two of my favorite girls," Damien exclaimed, speaking of his sister and Machumu.

Damien hugged Machumu. After he let her go, he reached out towards Nicole, who jumped to her feet and ran into his bear hug.

"Hey, big brother!"

"Baby girl," Damien began saying, "you didn't think your brother would miss this event, did you?"

"You better not have," Nicole stated.

They sparred playfully. Everyone looked at the skills both displayed. Their fluent motion showed it wasn't a game when it came down to it. Demetri observed everyone's facial expressions and smiled proudly.

"If those of you who don't know my niece and nephew are wondering, they have trained with the best in the country of the origin of several martial arts. You don't have to take my word for it. All you have to do is try their patience. But no one here is planning on doing such a dumb thing, so let's enjoy ourselves."

They ate and talked. During his entire time being with Nicole, Mark hadn't seen her so playful and talkative. But she still kept a watchful eye around the table, and he noticed her brother was doing the same. Demetri watched him observe the scene for a moment before excusing himself and asking him to join him.

"Okay, Nephew, what did you see?" Demetri asked Mark.

"My wife and her brother are very cautious around people they're not really familiar with. My instincts tell me it's more due to people's unlearned ways of the custom of this business and the rules they live by," Brad informed him.

Demetri stroked his chin, nodding his head to show approval. "And what do you think of Ted?"

"Eager and willing to take advice in order to get on top and stay there. For the short time I worked with him, he has shown improvement. He's all about what's good for business. A bright future, if molded into it," replied Mark.

Demetri continued to nod, considering everything. "Anything odd?"

Brad shook his head. "Not really, besides the fact my wife isn't too fond of Lil Will because of his expression when I introduced them."

Knowing his niece, and the fact her brother was there too, Demetri put his hand on his forehead. "Not good, Nephew."

"Why?" It dawned on Brad. "Oh boy."

Reality kicked in real quick.

The two men looked at each other and hurried back inside to join the feast. Demetri remained standing, staring at his niece and nephew as he addressed their guests.

"I'm sorry to have to inform you all that there has been a change of plans. Machumu, Ted, and Lil Will, you will not be staying tonight. A helicopter will fly you back to the airport, where you can pick up your vehicles. Before you all go, we shall get down to business.

"As some of you know, the mayor and sheriff in Albany are deceased. An election is about to be held for these positions. Ted here is going to become the new mayor, meaning, no more drug transactions for you, Ted. You have a clean record, and it's best we keep it that way.

"As for the sheriff position, it's still a work in progress. Lil Will, choose between Henry and Mike to be the person to handle transactions," Demetri stated.

Lil Will nodded. "Okay."

Demetri shook his head. "Not later, Lil Will. Now."

Lil Will thought for a moment. "In that case, Mike will handle the money transactions while Henry takes care of the shipment."

Demetri nodded approvingly. "Good. A lesson well learned. Know your assets for their skills, therefore, you allow them to show their loyalty. Now, finish eating and talking because tomorrow, some of you may not ever talk again."

On his way back out, Demetri gestured for his niece and nephew to follow. They met him in his study.

"Have a seat," Demetri said.

Nicole and Damien sat quietly.

"Damien, you may be naive or you may not be naive to what is on your sister's mind," Demetri stated curiously.

Damien looked at his uncle with a serious expression on his face. "It all depends on what you're referring to, Uncle."

"Her plans for one or two of our guests," Demetri replied before looking at his niece. "Do I need to say more, Nicole?"

Nicole frowned. "Uncle, I wasn't going to kill him. Maybe rough him up a little bit, but not kill him. As long as his brother stayed out of it, everybody would've survived."

Demetri couldn't help but laugh at her. "That means we would've had a dead future mayor and a dead head. That would've been tragic for business. Are we going to let them live, Nicole?"

She looked at her brother.

Demetri realized she really wanted to teach Lil Will a lesson. "No silent transmissions, Nicole. Look at me."

Nicole threw her hands up, frustrated. "Just keep him away from me, and we have a deal."

"Then it's settled," Demetri insisted. "How do you like your wedding gifts?"

Nicole's whole attitude changed. "We love them."

Seeing the mood had lightened up, Demetri smiled. "Let's return to our guests."

Demetri, Damien, and Nicole walked back into the banquet hall all smiles like death wasn't the topic of discussion just seconds ago.

Thaddeus stood and took the floor. "It's always a pleasure to have family together. This business doesn't or hasn't lasted this long just off of friendships and mutual goals. It's still here because of family. Let's keep it that way."

"I agree, brother. Now, the big moment. Nicole, Brad, please stand."

They stood up and joined Thaddeus at his side.

Thaddeus went on, saying, "This lovely couple will no longer be at your services. If you don't already know where they're living, you won't ever know. With that, I ask you all to say your farewells and be on your way."

Lil Will didn't quite understand what was going on around him. The only thing that had become clear in his mind was the reason the mayor and sheriff died. He pounded Mark up and embraced him. He hadn't told him where he was living, and he wasn't foolish enough to ask.

Mark and Nicole got on the helicopter and left. Six hours later, they were back home and in the bed. Lovemaking was out of the question. They were so exhausted from flying that sleep claimed them instantly.

Willie Slaughter

Chapter Eleven

The day had come. Mike, Teddy, Henry, T, and Lil Will waited on Dink to show up at Henry's crib. They had already come to the verdict. By the time the fifth blunt was being blazed, he arrived, and Lil Will gave it to him raw and uncut.

"Dink, we gon' keep shit plain and simple. Niggas ain't hearing yo' half-stepping bullshit. You a Slaughter Boy, but this money shit is deeper than blood ties my nigga. Either you all the way S.M.F., or ya ass is outta gas," Lil Will said coldly.

Dink nodded. "Bruh, I know I fucked up big time. The shit been eating at me since it happened. Even though we hit them niggas hard who did it, I still got murder on my mind. My nigga, on my life, I'm Slaughter Boy and S.M.F. fo' life."

"A'ight, bro," said Lil Will. "No more sideline hustling shit. We all gon' eat properly. T done came up with a fool-ass plan to make it happen."

T took the floor and told everyone what his plans was. It didn't take Dink long to do the math and add on to his plan. "So basically, we gon' be moving straight weight, which means we can send enough paperwork to cop three times the original shipment. Since we stepping on it twice, two will pay for three more. We all make good."

Lil Will nodded with a smile. "Now, that's the Dink I know. The next shipment is already on the way, so we'll test run it. T, how's the peace talk going?"

"I got the meeting set up fo' Friday," T informed Lil Will.

Lil Will nodded. "Good. The work will be here by then, and we will have time to cut it. Make sho' you tell them niggas to have their check right fo' whatever they trying to cop."

They sat around and kicked it for the rest of the day. Dink was at ease and glad to be back in good grace with his brothers.

***

Demetri, Thaddeus, Sis, and Mark were being entertained by Damien and Nicole. They were on the front lawn sparring with bow staffs. She had on a crimson red ninja suit and he wore a black one. Their movements were as fast as if it was real combat.

Mark observed the amusement on the others' faces as she went for a sweeping blow with the staff and he backward flipped to dodge the attack. They danced around for every bit of an hour. They dropped the staffs and began hand to hand combat. As far as he could tell, they were equally matched.

Looking at them train made him think about Lil Will, and the fact that the man didn't know his life was in so much danger the other day just because of an expression. Seeing both of them turning backward flips away from each other snapped him back to reality. On the last flip, they both threw ninja stars at each other, which they back dropped to dodge and bounded back to their feet. They bowed towards each other, and then turned, bowing to everyone watching.

Demetri, Thaddeus, and Sis jumped to their feet, giving them a standing ovation. He stood and clapped silently. All he could think of was the new life he was about to live.

***

Special Agent Sarah had led the agency to a major bust. A couple years ago, some wannabe Mexican cartel had moved in on an Italian territory, causing trouble. They'd overlooked the mishap until someone important was murdered. Now, the employers wanted blood for blood.

"Grab those two there," Sarah instructed the other agents. "I got this one."

She yanked the wannabe drug lord up on his feet. The tattoos on his face disgusted her. Seeing they weren't heading out to a patrol car, he started speaking in Spanish, asking her what she was doing. She answered him back in Spanish, telling him to shut the fuck up before she put a bullet in his skull. She pushed him into the bathroom and closed the door. Inside, she kicked him in the stomach, and as he doubled over, she kicked him again, causing his body to fall in the tub. She turned on the hot water. As it ran over his face, she screwed the silencer on the pistol and put two slugs in his head before walking out, closing the door behind her. Back at the office, she made a phone call.

"Hello," a lady answered.

Sarah smiled. "How's my daughter doing?"

"Great, Mom," she replied. "I hope you're not upset with me missing work today."

"Not at all," Sarah said sincerely. "Deliver a message for me."

"Sure. Hold on." Sarah's daughter handed the phone to the guy standing next to her. "It's my mother."

The guy took the phone, smiling as he said, "Hello?"

"That's settled," Sarah said.

The man sighed with relief. "Thank you. Keep it official business."

"Understood," Sarah stated and then hung up the phone.

***

Sopia and Sabrina were back in Atlanta, kicking it with Kerria. Like last time, they hit the mall on an all-out shopping spree. As they shopped, Sabrina filled Kerria in on the happenings in Albany. It all sounded like the usual until she brought up the news of Lil Will being back in town.

"Hold up. Who?" Kerria asked Sabrina.

Sabrina filled her in. "Yeah, homegirl, that nigga is back in The Good Life. Them niggas doing their thang."

Kerria nodded cautiously. "Sounds about right. Slaughter Boyz is what's happening. S.M.F. for life."

"Yeah, but ya know that nigga's a wanted man dead or alive. You ask me, he was dumb as hell showing up like some of them niggas and hoes ain't thinking 'bout cashing his ass in fo' that check," said Sabrina.

Kerria laughed nervously. "Different strokes for different folks. What you think about it?"

Sabrina looked at Kerrica sideways. "What I think 'bout what? Turning his ass in? A check is a check."

Kerrica looked at her in disbelief. She turned her attention to Sopia, who already knew what was on her mind. "Y'all excuse me. I got to hit the bathroom."

Kerrica entered the restroom. She waited until it was empty before making the call. The male voice answered on the other end. "What's up? Who is this?"

"It's Kerrica," she replied.

"What's good, cuz?"

"I'm straight. Listen, this bitch Sabrina is state property. How do I know? The bitch just told me and Sopia she'll cash Lil Will in for the paper. Handle that bitch, kinfolk. Bet."

Kerrica went on and used the restroom for real since she was already there. She caught up with them at the checkout aisle. Sopia already knew what was up.

"Say, Kerrica," Sopia began saying, "why don't we hit The Good Life and party tonight? I really ain't trying to bump into that nigga I met the last time when we were up here. I had to make him beat the pussy. He wanted to make love to it."

Kerrica laughed. "I'm down with that. Let me find out Mike got yo' ass tapped and you sprung on the dick."

Sopia looked up at the sky, thinking about what Kerrica had said. "Girl, if you only knew."

Kerrica stopped by her house before they left town. She dropped her merchandise off and let her husband know she was going to visit her cousins, and that she would be back in the morning.

Three hours later, they were in Albany sitting inside of Sabrina's apartment. The whole crew showed up to see Kerrica.

"Kerrica, what it do, kinfolk?" Henry said happily.

"Henry! Hey cuz," she replied.

They hugged.

When she saw Lil Will, tears poured from her eyes at the thought of Bee. Kerrica hugged him tight.

"Man, I'm sorry to hear about bruh."

"It's all good, Kerrica," Lil Will said hugging her back. "We rocked them niggas to sleep who did it. What's good though? How you been?"

"Living the good life, fo' real," she replied.

Henry was texting someone on the phone when Sabrina pulled up, trying to kiss him. He brushed her off and told her to chill out. That got a negative reaction out of her.

"Nigga, ya cousin down here, and yo' ass get all upper class on a bitch! Fuck you and her!"

He didn't respond. He kept texting until the message came back he was waiting for. It wasn't a good thirty seconds later when the knock came at the front door. Mad, Sabrina went and opened the door.

It was Machumu.

"What's up, girlfriend? That nigga Lil Will in here with the rest of them niggas," Sabrina said.

Machumu didn't say anything. She walked in and spoke to everyone politely.

"How is everyone doing? Will everyone please excuse themselves? I need to have a woman-to-woman talk with Miss Sabrina here."

Henry was already heading out the door, still texting. Kerrica, having an idea what was up, followed his lead, and Sopia was behind her. Everybody else was naive to the obvious, so she turned it up a notch.

"Either y'all niggas deaf or dumb! I said get the fuck up and leave! I ain't asking again!"

Lil Will, although dumbfounded, knew when she was serious. He told the rest of the crew to come on. As soon as the door closed, she commenced to kicking Sabrina's ass. She tried to get away from her, but it wasn't happening.

She beat her until she got tired and Sabrina was too bloody and bruised to fight back. Knowing she couldn't let her live, she pulled out a straight razor and slit her throat. "Tell that, bitch."

While she was walking out, the cleanup crew was walking in.

***

It was two-fifteen in the morning and Nicole and Mark were creeping through the woods behind their estate. Neither said a word until they reached the clearing that led to another estate.

Nicole pointed towards the estate and started explaining. "This estate belonged to our family for centuries. Then the Turks came in and murdered my great-grandfather."

Brad nodded as he looked at the place. "So, that's who owns it now?"

"No, they stole it," she replied coldly. "Spoils of war. We're going to take it back. Stay close."

They crept across the lawn without being seen. Posted beside one of the sheds, Nicole drew her long sword and he followed her lead. Three guards turned the corner. Their mistake was not having their fingers on the triggers.

She cut the first guard's throat and thrust the sword through the second. Mark stabbed the third guard in the chest and then slit his throat. She watched in admiration, thinking to herself how they were going to make love after this was over. After they dragged the dead bodies behind the shed, they crept on around to the back of the main house.

There were four guards standing on post. She motioned for him to stay put. He nodded.

She reached inside of her suit inner pocket and took out four ninja stars. Holding two in each hand, she rolled out and into a kneeling position and threw the stars, killing all four men at one time.

Nicole waved for him to come on. Crouched low, Brad made his way over to her side. Once there, she retrieved the stars and they drug the bodies and propped them up on the side of the house.

"No man or woman is to be left alive," Nicole warned Brad. "If you have a problem with killing women or children, now is the time to speak because once we enter this house, there's no turning back. Either we kill everyone and make it out alive, or die thinking morally. Understood?"

Brad nodded. "Lead the way."

Nicole kissed him on the lips. "I love you so much."

The door wasn't locked, so they entered with ease. All of the lights downstairs was out. She didn't need night vision goggles, but she put them on so he would know to put his on. Instead of pulling the long sword, they pulled the short blades as they crept through the house.

As they approached the stairs, footsteps could be heard coming down. They waited patiently in the shadows on the target to come in full view. Seeing the infrared view of the man, Brad crept behind him, and while clasping a hand over his mouth to muffle any sound, slit his throat. He laid the dead man on the floor away from the stairs. Nicole counted forty-five breaths to see if anyone else was on their way down.

No one came, so they silently and swiftly made their way up. The light was on in the hallway, and an armed guard stood smoking a cigar outside of a room door, where inside, laughter was heard. She waited for him to make the mistake she knew he would. The guard, tired of hearing the noises coming from inside the room, turned his back and started walking down the hall in the opposite direction of them. It was the moment she was waiting for. Without hesitation, she ran up behind him and stabbed him through the back of the neck. As he fell, she slit his throat to be on the safe side.

Before entering the room, where people were still up having fun, they went from room to room, slitting throats while they slept. No door was left unopened, nor did anyone behind them survive. They met back in the hallway in front of the door and took the night vision goggles off. She knocked on the door and started counting the distance between footsteps.

By the unbalanced sound of the footsteps, she knew whoever was coming to the door was under the influence, which normally meant it was the head of the estate room, and he was entertaining his wife or a whore or both.

When the door opened and they both stabbed him in the gut, she realized it was both. They started screaming, and she really didn't care anymore because they were the only ones still alive. She pulled out her long sword and butchered them unmercifully. With everyone dead inside and out, they sheathed their swords and took deep breaths.

Mark kissed Nicole. "By the way, I love you too."

She looked at him and smiled. "Oh, I know. Now, for the easy part." She made a phone call. "Hey Uncle. Yes, it's done. Oh yes, my husband's a natural. Okay. You too." She hung up and smiled at him. "Uncle said hi and welcome to the family. Not to mention that he loves us."

Mark nodded and looked around them. "Thanks. Now what about all these dead bodies?"

Before he could get the question out good, he heard vehicles approaching. He peeped out of an upstairs window and saw several vans pull up.

Nicole's smile faded away. She was back looking serious again. "There's the cavalry. We must get going. Just because they work for us doesn't mean they get to see us."

Nicole and Brad hurried out of the house and headed back through the woods.

"The first one gets to be on top," said Nicole. She took off at a sprint.

Mark didn't even attempt to outrun her. For one, he smoked too much, something he'd recently stopped, and two, he wanted her to be on top.

Back at the estate and in the shower they sexed each other, and after the shower, she rode him until they climaxed together and fell asleep.

***

A couple of months had gone by and morning had come. Mike did exactly what he had been told to do. He put on his double-breasted Ralph Lauren suit and went straight to the mayor's office. When he walked in, the receptionist asked him if he had an appointment. After giving her his name, she checked the calendar.

"I do apologize, sir," the secretary said. "Right this way please." She escorted him to Mayor Teddy's office.

When she opened the door, cameras, microphones, and recorders were aimed directly at him. The security had to clear a path for him to get through the door. Upon seeing him, the mayor smiled.

"Mr. Michael Coates, it seems due to your outstanding military profile and community standing, you've been nominated to fulfill the duty to the citizens of Albany, Georgia as their new sheriff. Are you willing to uphold this office of justice righteously? It's obvious the prior sheriffs have mistreated the people of middle and poverty class."

Mike responded professionally. "I will do my best, Mayor James."

"That's good news to the public, Mr. Coates," Mayor Teddy replied.

They went through the swear-in process. Afterwards, the mayor asked that he say a few words to the press for the public.

Mike faced the cameras with a serious look upon his face and said, "As your new sheriff, I will continue to assist with the rebuilding of Albany making it into the city where people would want to come live and visit. The level of criminal activity is already at an all-time low, but we're going to work harder to make it to where it is nonexistent. Thank you."

Teddy and Mike took a couple pictures together, which they knew without a doubt would be posted as the cover story of the newspaper.

***

Machumu and Sopia had become great friends. Certain cooking tips they learned from each other made the specials that much more special. They were just opening up for the day when Machumu's phone rang. She looked at the caller's ID and smiled.

"Say der mon. How ya doin'," Machumu said, answering her phone.

The caller sighed. "Ah, Machumu, must you do that to me?"

She laughed. "Hey, family. Just decided to spice up your day."

"In that case," the caller said, "one spice deserves another. The estate is yours."

"Come again," Machumu said, not believing what she'd heard.

The caller laughed. "The estate is yours. You can move into it this weekend."

She screamed. "Are you serious? Thank you! Thank you! Thank you!"

"Aye, what's family for? Leave the restaurant business to Sopia. She can handle it. I'm pretty sure with the currency flowing through our family you can open up a chain of restaurants over here," he said convincingly.

"You know I will. Thank you so much," Machumu replied happily.

"No problem. Just keep your hubby's head screwed on right and tight," was his response.

"I got you," she promised. They hung up.

She jumped to her feet, dancing. Sopia started dancing just because.

"Girl!" Machumu screamed as she grabbed Sopia by the hands, "I'm moving on up! This business is yours! You can have it!"

Sopia looked surprised. "What? Oh my God!"

They yelled together like two teenage girls going on their first dates.

**

Special Agent Sarah sat behind her desk, pretending to be looking over reports when she came across something interesting. She called Agent Harris in her office to examine the file.

Agent Harris read through the file carefully. "It seems we have a delicate situation here, Special Agent Sarah. Do we make the call, or do we make the call?"

"We make the call," replied Special Agent Sarah Harris.

Sarah dialed the number from her personal phone. It rang once, and the line was connected.

"Hello," Special Agent Sarah Harris said. "Are you aware of the investigation into Judge McBride for child molestation? No? Okay. Will do with pleasure." She hung up the phone. Sarah put her phone inside of her jacket pocket. "Agent Harris, let's go pay ole baby-raping McBride a visit."

Agent Harris threw the file down on top of the stack of files on the desk. "Ma'am, yes ma'am."

They rode together over to the judge's two story Victorian. Agent Harris knocked on the door. Nobody answered. It was obvious he was home because all of his vehicles were parked out front on display.

They tried the door. It was locked. Quickly, the young agent picked the lock and opened the door. They crept silently through the living room.

Slaughter Gang 2

When they reached the stairs that spiraled upward, they were able to hear faint whimpering sounds and grunts. With guns with silencers drawn, they rushed up the stairs and kicked in the door. The sight before them was disgusting. The judge was screwing a little boy and he was enjoying it.

Sarah shook her head with disgust. "You nasty son of a bitch!"

Special Agent Sarah snatched him off of the young boy, who couldn't have been any older than ten. Her partner grabbed the little boy and his clothes and carried him downstairs.

Agent Harris looked the little boy over. "Are you okay? Just get dressed and stay right here. He won't hurt you ever again. I promise."

With malice written all over her face, she ran back upstairs into the room. Without hesitation, she punched him in the mouth.

"I'm going to personally make sure you suffer before you die!"

The other agent was on the phone.

"Go ahead, okay." Sarah put her phone in inside jacket pocket.

"Mission confirmed. He's all yours, youngster. Make me proud."

Agent Harris popped her knuckles. "Oh with much pleasure."

She beat him senseless before tying him up. She took out her field knife and slowly castrated him. The screams were horrifying, but sounds of pure pleasure to them. Opening his mouth, she jammed his manhood inside before slitting his throat from ear to ear.

Sarah nodded approvingly. "Nice work, baby. Let's go. We'll take the boy back to the agency and run a check to find his parents."

They left, taking the child with them.

Chapter Twelve

Machumu and Lil Will had moved into their new home in Texas. It was a dream come true for her and a long time coming promise for him. He had brought his own security because everyone who was there left with Demetri and Thaddeus. S.M.F. had moved up.

His phone rang and he answered. "Hello?"

"Bruh, it's Mama's birthday. Did you forget?" Teddy reminded Lil Will.

"Hell nah, nigga. What kind of question is that? She on her way to me right now," replied Lil Will.

Teddy was surprised. "Yeah?"

Lil Will chuckled. "Yeah. Why, what's up?"

"That explains why her stuff is being moved by a moving company," Teddy replied.

"A'ight, bro. I'll get up with ya," Lil Will said.

As Lil Will hung up, the chopper was landing on the helipad. Two of the armed men helped her off the helicopter. As soon as her feet touched solid ground she dropped to her knees and kissed the grass. "Thank you, Jesus!"

Everyone laughed.

Lil Will walked over and personally escorted her inside. "Welcome home, Mama. Happy birthday," Lil Will said.

Ruby's eyes widened. "Oh my Lord! How will I ever find my way around this place?! Where's the kitchen?"

"Which one, Mama?" he replied laughing.

"Lord have mercy! How many kitchens is it?" she asked enthusiastically.

"Four kitchens, fifteen bedrooms, seven baths, and a lot more. Would you like a grand tour, Mama?" he asked.

She nodded. "Nope! I'll make my way around just fine."

She started walking off by herself. Everyone else went back to doing whatever they were doing before she arrived.

***

Dink, Henry, and T were the last ones left to keep the empire they'd built afloat. It was a real easy part to play. T had opened up a recording studio, and he had local talented rappers and singers to come through. They sat listening to the last youngster rapping when Henry's phone vibrated on the table.

"Yo. What's the biz?" Henry answered.

"What y'all up to, fam?" Mike said.

Henry turned the music down. "In the studio, fucking with T. Why, what's happening?"

"Any of 'em any good?" asked Mike.

"Hell yeah," Henry said with confidence.

"Throw a li'l amateur concert for The Good Life then. You know what to do," Mike said.

"A'ight, fam. We'll set that up for the near future," Henry replied.

"Bet that up, my guy. Tell the fam I said love," said Mike.

Henry bobbed his head to the track the rappers was laying down in the studio. "A'ight. One."

He hung up.

Henry told Dink and T what Mike said. They didn't have a problem with making it happen.

***

Mark and Nicole met Demetri and Thaddeus on the front porch of the old estate. There were no handshakes. They all hugged like family before walking inside.

"Home sweet home," Thaddeus said with a smile.

Demetri took a deep breath. "Brad, this is the estate where Thaddeus and I were born. Our father's father and his father built this place from the ground up with sweat, tears and much bloodshed. When the Turks came through, they tried to assist them with building something for themselves, but the bastards had a different plan. They killed the hands that attempted to help them, and that's the story of their undermining to takeover this wonderful estate."

"They won't be doing that again," Mark replied promisingly. Demetri nodded.

"Correct you are, Brad. Correct you are."

***

Sopia was doing great. She had her own business to run and was enjoying being a boss. One of the employees always kept an eye on her. Tanya was short, dark-skinned, natural hair, and a pretty smile. Everything that spelled sexy to Sopia.

She passed by and bumped up against her while looking over her shoulder smiling. It must've been cool because the young woman smiled back. After work, the young lady made sure she stayed behind. Tanya walked into the office and stood. "Sopia, do you have a minute?"

Sopia looked her over from head to toe. "Depends."

She walked on into the office. "I'll take that as a yes."

Tanya sat on top of the desk and opened her legs, revealing that she wasn't wearing any panties.

Sopia's mouth became watery. "I have all the minutes in the world." She licked her lips and dug in with her tongue.

Sopia gave her face like no other. The young lady laid flat on the table as she grabbed her inner thighs and tongued her pussy down.

"Oh baby. Oh baby. Yes. Yes," Tanya moaned while winding her hips.

Sopia came up for air. "You like that? You like it? Huh?"

"Yes... Oh yes," she replied, feeling fulfilled.

Sopia sucked her pussy from soaking wet to dry.

Feeling satisfied, she came up for air. Pulling her to her, they French kissed while she fingered her until she came.

"Mmm. You wanna come to my place tonight?" asked Sopia.

Tanya shrugged. "If you want me to."

Sopia licked her lips. "I'll love to have you over to be my dinner with your sexy ass." They closed up and left together.

At Sopia's apartment they started all over again, but this time naked. Her light-skinned body slid smoothly across Tanya's dark skin. They rubbed clitoris to clitoris, breast to breast, moaning in each other's ears until climaxing and falling asleep in each other's arms.

***

Lil Will and Machumu had just finished an erotic session of sexing when her phone lit up. Still breathing hard, she answered. "Hello? Hey! I see. 'Bout to handle it right now. Same to you."

She hung up, jumped out of the bed, and began dressing.

Machumu looked at Lil Will's exposed body and smiled, but he wasn't smiling. "Where you headed?" he asked.

She finished dressing. "Get your ass up and come on. We got work to do."

He frowned. "At twelve midnight, Mu?"

She laughed. "Yep. You still don't get it, do you? Living in luxury like this ain't free."

"You know money ain't an issue baby," Lil Will replied.

She started to laugh. She realized the love of her life was still wet behind the ears about certain things. "Baby boy, money don't pay for luxuries in the world we're a part of. Blood is the almighty dollar. Do you have any idea the blood that's been shed just to keep your ass alive and outta a cell? Nigga, you better wake up."

Machumu stood before him dressed in all-black, screwing a silencer on a rifle.

Lil Will realized she wasn't going to ask him again to get up and dressed. What he didn't know was what would've happened if he didn't. He jumped up and dressed in all black as well.

He grabbed his gun, but she told him it wasn't necessary.

"We ain't going into a street war, baby. What we do is called assassinations. Important people fuck up, and they get assassinated. Other important people take their place," she explained. She inspected the rifle, making sure the barrel was balanced and the scope was accurate.

Satisfied, they left. On their way to the destination, there was no exchange of words. It dawned on him that his misunderstanding irritated her. Almost an hour later, she pulled into a secluded area and hopped out without saying anything.

He got out and walked to the trunk, where she grabbed the rifle and two sets of night vision goggles.

Machumu gave Lil Will a set of the goggles. "Huh. This is all you'll need this time. I got the rest. Come on, and try not to make any noise."

As they crept through the woods, Lil Will was wondering to himself who would be up this late moving around to the point someone could pick them off with a sniper rifle.

When they reached the edge of the cliff and he looked at the house a good seventy-five yards away, his thoughts changed. Not only was someone up, they were actually making out on the patio.

He watched as Machumu setup and took aim.

"Don't watch me," she said while adjusting the scope. "Never take your eyes off the target."

Lil Will looked at her questioningly. "Who's the target?"

She didn't reply.

With a smirk on her face, she squeezed the trigger twice. The first bullet tore into the skull of the man, and the second hit the woman in the center of the chest.

"Everyone around the target becomes a target," she explained, looking at the dumbfounded expression on his face.

On the way back to the estate she made the call.

"Hello," she said as the line was connected. "Of course. You know I'll never let you down. Umm…a work in progress."

She laughed at whatever the person at the other end said. "Yep! Alright. Talk to you later. Bye."

Machumu put her phone on the dashboard.

It amazed Lil Will how quickly her demeanor changed. She was just laughing with whoever she talked to on the phone. Now, she was all serious-looking.

***

Special Agent Sarah and a team of agents were on a tear. Since she had made head of her division with Agent Harris second in command, the agency was functioning like the agency again. Raids happened and arrests were made. If it was any illegal dealings going on, no one would ever suspected it.

They stood out front in the parking lot of a Turkish-owned store, which they'd just raided and made a major drug bust.

Along with the store, they seized over thirty million dollars of hard cash and five hundred bricks of uncut Peruvian Flake.

"Great day, team," Sarah said, congratulating the agents. "Take these scumbags to their new residence. Agent Harris, I'm assuming you'll be joining me for lunch."

Agent Harris saluted her. "Ma'am, yes ma'am."

They left in an unmarked sedan.

At her lakefront home, the young agent took two brief-cases out of the trunk. At the raid, everyone was too busy enjoying doing police work to pay attention. It was originally forty-five million in hard cash.

Sarah smiled. "Baby girl, you definitely know how to make your mama proud."

"I learned from the best," she replied. "7.5 mill apiece is great retiring funds."

Sarah nodded in agreement. "Yep. We'll funnel it into our savings accounts a little at a time to keep down the suspicion. Anything particular you wanted to do for the rest of the day?"

Her daughter shook her head. "Nope, not really. Sit here with you looking out over the lake until sunset. Maybe sip on a Long Island Iced Tea or two while we plan the near future."

And that's what they did.

Mother and daughter sat together enjoying drinks while conversing and watching the sun set.

Willie Slaughter

Chapter Thirteen

It was 12 noon when Lil Will woke up. As he rolled over, he realized Machumu was already up and about somewhere. The woman was a real mystery, and a killer on top of everything else. After a shower, he made his way through the kitchen until finding his mother with the cooks, cooking up a storm.

"Alrighty then," Lil Will began to say. "Whatever y'all cooking, I'm sho' eating. It's smelling like some country cooking up in here."

His mother started laughing. "Boy, ya know Mama Ruby don't play in a kitchen. Gon' in there and have a seat wit'cha woman. We been up all morning filling each other out. That's a good woman ya got yo'self. Don't mess it up being stupid."

Lil Will grabbed a cold beer out of the refrigerator. "I know, Mama. I got you." He walked into the dining room.

Machumu was in the middle of a phone call. Her facial expression told him it was probably business, so he kissed her on the cheek and sat quietly and popped the top on the Natural Ice beer.

"Okay. That's great. Keep me posted. Always," she said before hanging up. She set the phone on the table.

Without saying a word, Machumu picked up the backpack that was on the floor next to her chair and tossed it to him.

Lil Will looked at it curiously. "What's this?"

She didn't respond.

He unzipped the backpack and emptied the contents onto the table. The files and bags of evidence, which had his name and alias written on them, lay before him. He flipped open the first file and spot read through it.

His eyes widened. "What the hell? Shit!" He was reading the second file.

With the ongoing investigation and evidence they had against him, there was no way he would've escaped natural life. But that wasn't all. Come to find out, Dink had been falling for the banana in the tailpipe.

Lil Will rubbed his head. "Dammit, man! A nigga really never had a fighting chance!"

"Nope," she replied between eating grapes. "That's why you need to do more listening than thinking you run shit."

He blew her a kiss. "Thank you, baby."

Machumu looked at him seriously. "Consider it my premarital gift to you. And it's the only one you getting."

He laughed so hard that it brought tears to his eyes. He knew there was a possibility she wasn't joking, but her sense of humor was undeniable.

Finally, the cooks and his mother started strolling in carrying dishes of food. They all sat and ate.

"So, when's the wedding? I know y'all ain't gon' shack up. And if ya thought y'all was, not with Mama Ruby staying up in here. I need grandbabies," Ruby said, looking at her son.

Lil Will sat the fork down on the plate. "Speaking of grandchildren. Dee and her son moving in too."

"When?" his mother asked.

Lil Will looked at his Rolex to check the time. "They on the way now."

"What about yo' sistas and brothas? Are they coming too?" she asked.

Lil Will shook his head and laughed. "Excuse my language, but hell no. Besides, Teddy is a mayor, and Dink is an entrepreneur."

Ruby nodded. "Okay. Baby, I see ya point. But when did he become an entrepreneur? Or is that the political correct term for hustler?"

Everybody at the table burst into laughter. Even Machumu couldn't help herself. She actually choked from laughing so hard.

Lil Will nodded. "Yeah, Mama, something like that." They finished their brunch.

Machumu excused herself. She kissed him and hugged her future mother-in-law before leaving to take care of business. He wanted to go with her, but fought the urge, remembering her words. While she was gone, he took the backpack and destroyed it with the files and evidence inside. He stood in deep thought while watching it burn to ashes.

***

The Fox was jumping. For the first time in history, all sides were in the building and a fight hadn't broken out. "Cha Cha Slide" was bumping loud through the speakers, and every bad and not so fine female was on the dance floor going in. Dink, Henry, and T sat in VIP surrounded by S.M.F.

They were enjoying the entertainment. Once the song went off, T jumped up and strolled out and over to the DJ.

"Watch yaself young G! Let me have this fo' a minute," T yelled over the music to the DJ.

"A'ight, old school," he yelled back.

The DJ stepped to the side as T grabbed the mic.

"A'ight, Good Life! We got some talent off up in here tonight! Slaughter Boyz Inc. presents G Shot and his new single "G Shyt"!"

The rapper hit the stage flowing. Everybody hit the floor bopping, mopping, and juking.

The night flew by for Dink. *That's what happens when everybody's having fun*, he thought to himself.

Sopia and her chick Tasha were on the dance floor drunk, feeling freaky. They danced, rubbing all over each other. T noticed it and had the spotlight shining on them.

"Ah shit now! It's 'bout to go down! The Fox 'bout to get its first taste of real live finger-licking good! Do y'all thing, ladies!"

Without any shame, they tongued each other down while stripping. All of the hustlers had gathered around, chunking fifties and hundreds at them.

"A'ight, pimps and playas! You toss it, it's theirs! Pay fo' what ya wanna see," T yelled over the mic.

Everyone around was yelling, "Take it off!"

The girls obliged them. Down on the floor, with Sopia on top, Tasha licked her from the back as she sucked on her clit from the front. Money was laying all around them, and the men and some women were still tossing money on them.

About to cum, Sopia turned around and they French kissed while rubbing against one another until they came.

T was hyped up. "Now, that's a party! Don't do 'em no small favors!"

The rapper had left the stage. Feeling the vibe, Henry and Dink walked up to the DJ booth and requested a song.

T got on the mic. "A'ight, pimpettes and pimps! Play-erettes and playas! We 'bout to take y'all back to black in the days!"

The song, *Play at Your Own Risk*, bumped hard inside the club. Now all the old schools hit the floor with the youngsters. They started doing the bump, two-stepping and four-cornering. It was definitely a party. At the end of the night, everyone left the club feeling good.

***

She had driven all the way from South Texas to North Texas. Finally, she reached her destination. Checking the time, she saw that it was 1 a.m. Not that time really mattered. The great thing about her target was, she was pretty much a recluse. She stayed alone because of paranoia, which more than likely stemmed from the fact that she had crossed the wrong people - the exact reason she was picking the lock on the back door.

She entered the dark house quietly. She pulled out the pistol with the silencer on it and patiently crept through the house checking every room to make sure she left no stone unturned, so to speak. Assessing that her target was alone, she focused all of her attention on completing the mission.

The woman lay sound asleep in her king-sized bed. She crept over to the head of the bed and let two rounds off into the sleeping woman's face. Job done, she made her way back to the car and left.

***

Lil Will woke up the next morning being showered with kisses. Machumu snatched the covers off of him and straddled him.

"I'm glad the man downstairs is up and ready," Machumu said seductively.

"Machumu, where the hell you been?" Lil Will asked.

She started grinding on top of him. "No time for q and a, baby. Just enjoy the ride."

Where usually it would be a gentle lovemaking ordeal, it was a she fucked him good, hard, and a long time. She definitely knew how to change the subject along with his thoughts. He held on as long as he could before he released. Feeling him explode inside of her motivated her to grind harder and faster.

She moaned and screamed louder and louder as she came closer to her release. When the orgasm came, it shook her entire body. Without saying a word, she collapsed on top of him and was instantly asleep. He moved her off top of him and got up.

He went on about his usual day. He called his brothers to see how everyone and business was doing. Dee and his nephew had already arrived, so he knew they were good. He spent most of his day walking around in his own head. Around four, he made his way to the kitchen to see what his mother and the cooks were preparing for the evening meal.

He saw Machumu had gotten out of bed and was sitting at the table drinking coconut juice straight from a coconut. "Have a seat, Mr. James."

"What, you 'bout to lecture me again?" he asked in a sarcastic tone of voice.

"Aw, you so cute when you mad," she teased.

Lil Will couldn't help but laugh. "Go 'head on with the bullshit, girl."

"Will... Hold on," she said as her phone rang. She answered it. "Yes, it was easy. No problems. You're welcome. Give 'em a week? Okay. Goodbye." She put the phone down and sighed.

"What, another night out?" he said coldly.

Machumu looked at him sideways. "Listen, baby. I don't know what you think this is, but I can tell you what it ain't. This ain't a game you decide to play and stop playing when you feel like it. When you in, you in for life."

Lil Will was confused. "Well, what use is it to make it to the top?"

She laughed. "Baby, my love, even the so-called queen and can get pushed. The head ain't no better than the pawn. Nigga, we ain't exempt."

At that moment, he understood what he had to do. He took out his phone and made a call.

"Fam, what's good?" Lil Will said while looking at Machumu.

"Clocking dollars, bro. What up? Talk to me," Teddy replied.

Lil Will continued to stare Machumu in the eyes. "Shit really. Just calling to let y'all know I'm going off the radar. If I need ya, I'll contact ya, but don't try to call me."

"What's going on, bro?" Teddy asked out of concern.

"Nothing, my nigga. It's time we play the game like it's meant to be played," Lil Will answered

"A'ight, bro. Love, fam."

"Fo' sho'. Slaughter Boyz fo' life."

He broke his phone.

She looked at him and smiled. "Now, you're ready to play the game."

That was a fact that could not be denied. Lil Will was ready for whatever. Or was he? The streets was surely about to test that ass.

TO BE CONTINUED...
Slaughter Games 3
Coming Soon

Submission Guideline

Submit the first three chapters of your completed manuscript to ldpsubmissions@gmail.com, subject line: Your book's title. The manuscript must be in a .doc file and sent as an attachment. Document should be in Times New Roman, double spaced and in size 12 font. Also, provide your synopsis and full contact information. If sending multiple submissions, they must each be in a separate email.

Have a story but no way to send it electronically? You can still submit to LDP/Ca$h Presents. Send in the first three chapters, written or typed, of your completed manuscript to:

LDP: Submissions Dept
Po Box 870494
Mesquite, Tx 75187

DO NOT send original manuscript. Must be a duplicate.

Provide your synopsis and a cover letter containing your full contact information.

Thanks for considering LDP and Ca$h Presents.

Slaughter Gang 2

Coming Soon from Lock Down Publications/Ca$h Presents

BOW DOWN TO MY GANGSTA

By **Ca$h**

TORN BETWEEN TWO

By **Coffee**

BLOOD STAINS OF A SHOTTA **III**

By **Jamaica**

STEADY MOBBIN **III**

By **Marcellus Allen**

BLOOD OF A BOSS **VI**

By **Askari**

LOYAL TO THE GAME **IV**

LIFE OF SIN **III**

By **T.J. & Jelissa**

A DOPEBOY'S PRAYER **II**

By **Eddie "Wolf" Lee**

IF LOVING YOU IS WRONG... **III**

By **Jelissa**

TRUE SAVAGE **VII**

By **Chris Green**

BLAST FOR ME **III**

DUFFLE BAG CARTEL **IV**

By **Ghost**

ADDICTIED TO THE DRAMA **III**

By **Jamila Mathis**

A HUSTLER'S DECEIT 3

KILL ZONE **II**

BAE BELONGS TO ME III

SOUL OF A MONSTER II

By **Aryanna**

THE COST OF LOYALTY **III**

By **Kweli**

SHE FELL IN LOVE WITH A REAL ONE **II**

By **Tamara Butler**

RENEGADE BOYS **III**

By **Meesha**

A GANGSTER'S SYN II

By **J-Blunt**

KING OF NEW YORK V

RISE TO POWER III

COKE KINGS III

By **T.J. Edwards**

GORILLAZ IN THE BAY IV

De'Kari

THE STREETS ARE CALLING II

Duquie Wilson

KINGPIN KILLAZ IV

STREET KINGS 2

PAID IN BLOOD 2

Hood Rich

SINS OF A HUSTLA II

ASAD

TRIGGADALE III

Elijah R. Freeman
MARRIED TO A BOSS III
By Destiny Skai & Chris Green
KINGZ OF THE GAME III
Playa Ray
SLAUGHTER GANG III
By Willie Slaughter
THE HEART OF A SAVAGE II
By Jibril Williams
FUK SHYT II
By Blakk Diamond
THE DOPEMAN'S BODYGAURD II
By Tranay Adams

<u>Available Now</u>
<u>RESTRAINING ORDER **I & II**</u>
By **CA$H & Coffee**
<u>LOVE KNOWS NO BOUNDARIES **I II & III**</u>
By **Coffee**
<u>RAISED AS A GOON I, II, III & IV</u>
<u>BRED BY THE SLUMS I, II, III</u>
<u>BLAST FOR ME I & II</u>
<u>ROTTEN TO THE CORE I II III</u>
<u>A BRONX TALE I, II, III</u>
<u>DUFFEL BAG CARTEL I II III</u>

By **Ghost**

LAY IT DOWN **I & II**

LAST OF A DYING BREED

BLOOD STAINS OF A SHOTTA I & II

By **Jamaica**

LOYAL TO THE GAME

LOYAL TO THE GAME II

LOYAL TO THE GAME III

LIFE OF SIN I, II

By **TJ & Jelissa**

BLOODY COMMAS I & II

SKI MASK CARTEL I II & III

KING OF NEW YORK I II,III IV

RISE TO POWER I II

COKE KINGS I II

By **T.J. Edwards**

IF LOVING HIM IS WRONG…I & II

LOVE ME EVEN WHEN IT HURTS I II III

By **Jelissa**

WHEN THE STREETS CLAP BACK I & II III

By **Jibril Williams**

A DISTINGUISHED THUG STOLE MY HEART I II & III

LOVE SHOULDN'T HURT I II III IV

RENEGADE BOYS I & II

By **Meesha**

A GANGSTER'S CODE I &, II III

A GANGSTER'S SYN

By J-Blunt

PUSH IT TO THE LIMIT

By **Bre' Hayes**

BLOOD OF A BOSS **I, II, III, IV, V**

By **Askari**

THE STREETS BLEED MURDER **I, II & III**

THE HEART OF A GANGSTA I II& III

By **Jerry Jackson**

CUM FOR ME

CUM FOR ME 2

CUM FOR ME 3

CUM FOR ME 4

CUM FOR ME 5

An **LDP Erotica Collaboration**

BRIDE OF A HUSTLA **I II & II**

THE FETTI GIRLS **I, II& III**

CORRUPTED BY A GANGSTA I, II III, IV

By **Destiny Skai**

WHEN A GOOD GIRL GOES BAD

By **Adrienne**

THE COST OF LOYALTY

By Kweli

A GANGSTER'S REVENGE **I II III & IV**

THE BOSS MAN'S DAUGHTERS

THE BOSS MAN'S DAUGHTERS II

THE BOSSMAN'S DAUGHTERS III

THE BOSSMAN'S DAUGHTERS IV

THE BOSS MAN'S DAUGHTERS **V**

A SAVAGE LOVE **I & II**

BAE BELONGS TO ME I II

A HUSTLER'S DECEIT I, II, III

WHAT BAD BITCHES DO I, II, III

SOUL OF A MONSTER

By **Aryanna**

A KINGPIN'S AMBITON

A KINGPIN'S AMBITION **II**

I MURDER FOR THE DOUGH

By **Ambitious**

TRUE SAVAGE

TRUE SAVAGE II

TRUE SAVAGE **III**

TRUE SAVAGE **IV**

TRUE SAVAGE **V**

TRUE SAVAGE **VI**

By **Chris Green**

A DOPEBOY'S PRAYER

By **Eddie "Wolf" Lee**

THE KING CARTEL **I, II & III**

By **Frank Gresham**

THESE NIGGAS AIN'T LOYAL **I, II & III**

By **Nikki Tee**

GANGSTA SHYT **I II &III**

By **CATO**

THE ULTIMATE BETRAYAL

Slaughter Gang 2

By **Phoenix**

BOSS'N UP **I , II & III**

By **Royal Nicole**

I LOVE YOU TO DEATH

By **Destiny J**

I RIDE FOR MY HITTA

I STILL RIDE FOR MY HITTA

By **Misty Holt**

LOVE & CHASIN' PAPER

By **Qay Crockett**

TO DIE IN VAIN

SINS OF A HUSTLA

By **ASAD**

BROOKLYN HUSTLAZ

By **Boogsy Morina**

BROOKLYN ON LOCK I & II

By **Sonovia**

GANGSTA CITY

By **Teddy Duke**

A DRUG KING AND HIS DIAMOND I & II III

A DOPEMAN'S RICHES

HER MAN, MINE'S TOO I, II

CASH MONEY HO'S

By **Nicole Goosby**

TRAPHOUSE KING **I II & III**

KINGPIN KILLAZ I II III

STREET KINGS

169

Willie Slaughter

PAID IN BLOOD
By **Hood Rich**
LIPSTICK KILLAH **I, II, III**
CRIME OF PASSION I & II
By **Mimi**
STEADY MOBBN' **I, II, III**
By **Marcellus Allen**
WHO SHOT YA **I, II, III**
Renta
GORILLAZ IN THE BAY **I II III**
DE'KARI
TRIGGADALE I II
Elijah R. Freeman
GOD BLESS THE TRAPPERS I, II, III
THESE SCANDALOUS STREETS I, II, III
FEAR MY GANGSTA I, II, III
THESE STREETS DON'T LOVE NOBODY I, II
BURY ME A G I, II, III, IV, V
A GANGSTA'S EMPIRE I, II, III, IV
THE DOPEMAN'S BODYGAURD
Tranay Adams
THE STREETS ARE CALLING
Duquie Wilson
MARRIED TO A BOSS... I II
By Destiny Skai & Chris Green
KINGZ OF THE GAME I II
Playa Ray

SLAUGHTER GANG I II
By Willie Slaughter
THE HEART OF A SAVAGE
By Jibril Williams
FUK SHYT
By Blakk Diamond

Willie Slaughter

BOOKS BY LDP'S CEO, CA$H

TRUST IN NO MAN
TRUST IN NO MAN 2
TRUST IN NO MAN 3
BONDED BY BLOOD
SHORTY GOT A THUG
THUGS CRY
THUGS CRY 2
THUGS CRY 3
TRUST NO BITCH
TRUST NO BITCH 2
TRUST NO BITCH 3
TIL MY CASKET DROPS
RESTRAINING ORDER
RESTRAINING ORDER 2
IN LOVE WITH A CONVICT

Coming Soon
BONDED BY BLOOD 2
BOW DOWN TO MY GANGSTA

Slaughter Gang 2